Dedicated to my long-lost brother Larry who I can only hope has been happy since he disappeared in 1979.

I could have titled this book:

The Man and the Myth

Larry's Life Matters

A Work of Magical Realism

By

Jim Goodman

This novel is mainly fictional. Most of the events and characters described herein are imaginary and are not intended to refer to a specific place or person. The opinions expressed in this manuscript are solely the opinions of the authors. The author has represented and warranted full ownership/or legal right to publish all the material in this book.

Larry's Life Matters

Larry's Life Matters

ACKNOWLEDGEMENTS

It was with the support and good humor of much my family and many of my friends that this book was completed. First and foremost, my brother Don gave me much of the real information on Larry. He has had to put up with me longer than anyone else especially with my consistent questioning during this project. He also has a major role in the book as do many friends who gave me permission to use their real names. My stepsisters, Meri and Margie, have also put up with me for many years and both have played an instrumental role in the putting together of the book. Meredith Schorr (Meri) is an accomplished author in the chick-lit genre and she got me going in the right direction from the very beginning of this project while Margie's compassion has been an example to me for most of my adult life. Their mother Susan Schorr, my "Wicked stepmother", has been an inspiration as well and has prodded me along with imaginary kicks in the butt in real life as well as in the book. My friends Ben Steinlage and Burt Walker, also authors, helped me immensely with everything from critiques to the cover (Ben) to being a character in the book (Burt). Burt also set me up with his editor, Sabrina Jean, who was a great help in getting my writing in line. My ex-newspaper editor and sci-fi author, Rory McClannahan, also pointed out some flaws in my writing from the book's onset. But I probably would never have met him or my previous editors without Garry Wolfe. He was one of my professors when I returned to college in 2004 and he instilled a confidence in me to finally embark on the writing career I should have begun years earlier. It takes a real sense of humor to put up with me for decades as a lot of my friends have. But all of them also trusted me enough to use their real names in the book. From major characters like Wayne and Don Trimarchi as well as my high school friends who helped mold my humor had more minor roles in flashbacks: Kim Mühlhahn, Lee Rubin, Mark Pascale, Ricky Siegel and Amy Wertheim. And nothing would have been possible without my late parents, Abraham and Mazie Goodman or my late best friend, Jack Dautel, and his family including his ex-wife, Linda. This book was written mainly in their son Boomer's junkyard office. Jack's late parents, Rudy and Dottie Dautel, were two people who kept me from disappearing like Larry did back in the seventies.

FOREWORD

It has been a long hard road figuring out what happened to my brother Larry after he left my mother's apartment in January, 1979 at age sixteen. This book is being used as a tool in the search which I am doing concurrently with the writing of this book. As we speak, I am waiting for results of a DNA test which will possibly link me up with my brother's unidentified body or, in a better case scenario, find him institutionalized somewhere. A major portion of the profits from the book, if there are any, would go to a reward for a person who might help me find him or a donation to a missing persons agency. The facts stated about Larry in the first chapter of this book are true. The remainder is mostly fictional except for most of the flashbacks. The book is an account of what might have happened if I reconnected with Larry in 1989. That is, if you believe in fairy godfathers. The book is historical fiction with a twist or two. Most of the characters are at least a little crazy, the author included, and the crazy one does not live in the physical world. I have used many real names with permission of the owners but there are some characters who are purely based in fiction. I do most of my reading in the bathroom so the book has mainly short chapters. Just a few over 1,000 words. I hope that you enjoy it enough to read it straight through but please do not do so while sitting on the toilet. I can not be responsible for hemorrhoids or any other complications you might get if you don't switch to a more comfortable seat. The book is a mixture of where I grew up (New York/New Jersey) and where I felt like I should have grown up (New Mexico).Thus there is a sprinkling of Yiddish and a little Spanish used in the book. Nothing that an online dictionary would have trouble with. There is also a little Yinglish and a little Spanglish thrown in for good measure. My parents are both long gone but I hope they can rest in a little more peace if I can find out what happened to their youngest son.

Chapter 1

September 1989 — The 100th Interview, or so It Seemed:

I have never been one to like cities but there was something about them in the early morning before the streets are packed with people, cars and the combined cacophony of jackhammers and sirens. The city streets seem more peaceful before the Strip awakens in Vegas or when everyone's recovering from last night before hitting Bourbon Street in New Orleans. Even downtown Albuquerque.

It was just such a quiet day on New York City's Times Square when a siren broke it up.

I was nervous as the cop pulled me over but didn't think it showed by the time the New York City officer ambled up to my window. I had just bought my van and didn't know if there might be some weed in it from the previous owner.

His dog was barking in the car. "That's all I need is for his canine to be a drug dog and start sniffing around," I said to myself.

"Licensia, registration and insuranco," the cop said, having seen my New Mexico license plate and obviously not knowing that we are a part of the same country as New York is.

I laughed politely, not wanting to piss the cop off. "Yo tengo Ingles," I said.

"Huh," the cop said.

"I speak English," Correcting him on his geography didn't seem like a good idea at the time and he quickly received my documentation.

"You know you made a right turn on that last red light, young man."

"Yeah, I've been doing that since I moved out west in 1976 from Jersey. Didn't y'all make that legal here now too?"

"It's legal everywhere except here in the city, sir."

"Shoot, I'm very sorry. Didn't know that at all," I actually did but thought that I could get away with it since I had the New Mexico plate and license.

"What are you doing in our fair city today?"

"I'm visiting my dad out in Rockland but thought about seeing if there was any progress on finding my long-missing brother." I showed him a picture of my brother Larry at a Jet football game.

"You a Jet fan, too?"

I knew that the wrong answer could get me into a lot of trouble but I had no clue whether he was a Giant fan or not. The Giants had just won the Super Bowl three years earlier and were still doing better than the Jets so I lied.

"No, heck no, L.T. and Phil Simms all the way!"

I had obviously guessed right by the smile on his face. The son of a bitch was probably a Jet fan when they won the Super Bowl in '69 but just liked to be with a winning team.

"Hold on, I'll be right back," the cop said.

He went back to his car, probably checking on whether my car was stolen or I was wanted for any crimes or had warrants.

"No warrants or APBs on me?" I said as he approached my car with the paperwork making its way towards me. Fifteen years earlier, there might have been. "Guess they're all expired."

"No, you came up clean. I won't give you a ticket today but follow me back to the precinct."

Ooh, shit. I thought. Was he going to have his dog sniff through the car? Was he worried that I was a Mexican *coyote* (people smuggler) or drug smuggler?

***

"Just park here, you won't have to worry about anyone breaking into your car here," the cop said as we pulled up in front of the police station.

Damn, he's probably gonna' have someone or his dog search the van while I'm in there. I thought to myself.

"Come on in, nothing to worry about. You see, I had a sister go missing a while back and I know what I went through. So I wanted to help you," the cop said.

"Did you ever find her?" I asked while reading his badge, number 621-Murphy.

"We did. She was kidnapped by a cult in '79 but we rescued her."

"That could have been what happened to my brother; he disappeared in '79 too."

***

He led me to Interview Room One. "Just wait here a minute."

A tall, plain-suited detective with a slight paunch entered a couple of minutes later.

"Hi, I'm Sergeant Ronnie Fairgate with the Missing Persons Unit. I heard from Officer Murphy that you had a missing brother."

"Good to meet you." Noting that Fairgate had a body language that put you at ease, my hand quickly extended to meet his. "Yeah, my brother went missing around January 19 or 20, 1979. His sixteenth birthday was on the seventh and he said he was going to the Super Bowl from Park Ridge, New Jersey."

I had become accustomed to offering as much information in each sentence while talking to police about my brother Larry. "The game was on January 21 in Miami between Pittsburgh and Dallas, one of my least favorite Super Bowls between two of my least favorite teams. Larry had brown hair, brown eyes and was six feet, one inch tall and a hundred and eighty pounds; he played football at Park Ridge."

Fairgate let out a slight chuckle. "Yeah, not my favorites either. He took clothes with him...or money? So was he reported missing in Park Ridge?"

"Yeah, he was reported but all of the records are gone. We don't know what he took with him. Anyway, Larry or, officially Lawrence Jon Goodman, had run away once before. When he returned, he said he'd been living in the Greyhound station in Pittsburgh, cleaning buses and living in them. He returned with suitcases full of clothes and had become a Steeler fan in the days of Terry Bradshaw, Franco Harris and Lynn Swann."

"So, if he went, he may have gone by bus? And you were a witness to all this?"

"Actually, all the information I have is secondhand since I had moved to New Mexico in late 1976. My family had lived in Hillsdale, New Jersey but my parents lost their house and separated in 1975. My mom moved to 159 Maple Ave. in Park Ridge and my father to 500 Linwood Ave. in Fort Lee."

"Yes, sir, I'm familiar with Bergen County. Park Ridge has its own high school but is surrounded by other towns that all go to Pascack Hills or Pascack Valley."

"Oh, didja live out there? Yeah, so, even though Larry moved less than five miles after middle school, he went to Park Ridge High School as opposed to his two older brothers."

"No, I never lived or worked there. Just know some other police personnel out there. So what are all three brothers' names and where were they born?"

"Lawrence Jon Goodman was born at Mid-Island Hospital in Long Island to Mazie Georgianna (Kash) Goodman and Abraham Goodman. Donald David (Don) Goodman was born April 6, 1958 at White Plains Memorial and I, Jamie Saul Goodman, was born in White Plains on July 10, 1956. We moved from there to Massapequa in 1959."

"And when did you move to...uh... Park Ridge? Or Hillsdale, I mean?"

"My father had a small marketing company in Fort Lee and was driving from the Island to there for a couple of years. But we moved in my sophomore year, the end of 1971."

"And your parents are still alive?"

"My mother died in '82 but dad lives in Rockland, Spring Valley." I showed him the picture of Larry at around fifteen.

"Oh, a Jet fan, huh. I won't hold that against you," he laughed. "Any hobbies besides cheering for the wrong football teams?"

I laughed too. "Larry collected pennies as a kid and he would still remember the most valuable one, a 1909 VDB. My youngest brother also was a WW II expert who pored through collections of books on the subject."

"Any drug use that you know of?"

"I had heard from Don that Larry got into marijuana and possibly a little LSD not long before he took off in 1979. That was also noted in a diary which has since been lost."

"I'll see if there's any new information on this case, just keep in touch." He gave me his card.

"Thanks for your help." I didn't say it to him but I was thinking...just another dead end.

Chapter 2

In Which Larry is Found:

"If you won't give me a buck, then give me all your money, mother fucker," the oversized panhandler said. He pulled a large knife out of the pocket of the jacket that he obviously had slept in.

I guess it was a mistake not throwing him a couple of quarters when he had asked and gone on my way. But my mind was in other places as my investigation had come to what was one more dead end in the decade-long search for my brother.

It was in the dead end alley where my attacker wheeled with the glistening stiletto from his pocket.

"Here, take my money. You don't have to stab me," I yelled, reaching for the knife with my other hand.

He reached out his hand to grab the forty-six dollars I held out as a Boone's Farm bottle, that a man in the shadows had been drinking out of smashed across the back of his head. It surprised me as much as it surprised him when the bum jumped into the light.

But I still recognized the Boone's Farm container since my friends and I used to share bottles at age thirteen when I first started drinking. It only took us one bottle between the four of us for Chris, Mike, Kevin and I to get the sufficient charge.

"Good, I got him. He should be out for a few minutes," my savior said.

"Thanks, I'll go call the cops and an ambulance," I told him. "Say, I'm Jim, what's your name."

"It's not important. But I'll stay with him until you come back. Make sure he doesn't wake up and get away."

So I hurried down the dimly-lit street and, by the lights of a passing cab, soon found a pay phone.

I returned to find the vigilante wiping some of the blood from the still-dripping gash on the robber's face. He jumped up when he saw me.

"I've gotta' go. You called 9-1-1?" the mysterious man in the shadows said.

"Ye-." He darted down the dark alley almost before he heard my answer.

"He should still be out for a few more minutes," my rescuer yelled back over his shoulder as he scrambled away, half-looking for any other witnesses or first responders.

The panhandler was starting to come to a little bit and I took over wiping the blood off his face since his hands were tied. The sirens were getting closer as I got a strange feeling like I might know the robber.

The more blood that came off his face, the more his features came out. It was…it was my first girlfriend from Long Island.

Obviously, Ron had become Ronnie and he, or she, hadn't recognized me because my face had gained a few years and my body even a few more pounds. Or Veronica was just drunk.

But there still seemed like something else strange was going on. What had made Ron change in the last…well, I guess it had been twenty years?

In those two decades, I had moved from Massapequa in Long Island to graduate high school in Northern New Jersey and then, moved to New Mexico. Maybe her family problems in Massapequa were as bad as mine in Hillsdale, NJ but she had decided not to run across the country like I had.

Veronica was probably running from herself when she became a himself.

But who was the bottle-wielding man who had saved me from possibly being stabbed?

Oh well, the cops and EMTs were here now and it looked like Veronica had to go to the hospital.

"I'm not going to press charges," I told the cops, explaining the whole background to them. "What hospital is sh…he going to?"

The EMTs yelled that they were taking him to Bellevue, where most of the indigent and transient population were treated in Manhattan.

The police wanted to know more about the person who had smashed 'Ronnie' or Veronica with the bottle and I said that his features were hidden and he'd just acted mysteriously, even for a vigilante.

From my teen years talking cops out of tickets (although I got my share in my '68 Charger) to winning a court case where I was charged with assault and battery with an ice cream cone, I had a way of convincing those in authority of my side of the story being the truth.

"I was walking east on 32nd when what seemed to be just another panhandler approached me for 'some change'. I ignored him…er, her only to have him jump out in front of me, pulling a stiletto from his pocket."

"So that's when the vigilante came out of the shadows and bonked him on the head," the cop asked.

"Yeah, after I stuck some money out with my left hand and reached for the knife with my right. Then the other bum hit him with the apple wine bottle and I ran around the corner to call 9-1-1."

"And you got no real look at this vigilante. Not even an approximate height, weight or the clothing?"

"No, he was probably about six feet tall, a little taller than me, but his baggy, worn denim jacket concealed his weight. A scraggly Yankees cap covered his face."

"Alright, let me get your ID and phone number before I let you go," he said while handing me his business card.

All I could think of was Murphy's Law when I looked at Officer Pete Murphy's name on the business card.

16

***

Some strange urge was drawing me to the emergency room to see how my mugger was doing but by the time I found out where she...he was, he had bumped and run past me in the hall. Well, I guess that wasn't meant to be for more than one reason.

"Check your wallet?" A then unknown man asked me as I was leaving the ER. "How you doing otherwise?"

"Who doing...wait, who are you?" I asked, slightly recognizing my questioner from somewhere. Sometimes it seemed like I was four different people living reincarnated lives in different parts of these great United States.

And I couldn't place which life this person was from. But I did find my wallet. Luckily I kept a spare one which was left empty just to fool pickpockets.

"Didn't you go visit that tranny who tried to stab you last night?" the man who saved me said. "And the bitch got your wallet, huh?"

"Oh, thanks again for your help and it was just a spare empty wallet. I didn't think I'd see you again. Wait, how'd you know that was a transsexual?"

"No Adam's apple, boobs cut off," he said. "Upon further examination, I found no nuts where they should be. Always looking for new friends."

"Each to his own, didn't think I'd see you again after you took off into the shadows."

"Yeah, no fuckin' pigs around now. Let's just say we don't get along," he said. "I've got a few arrests in my past."

"Who are you?"

"You've known me your whole life but you haven't seen me much since you were five. I gotta' go; can't stay in one place too long."

He turned the corner as quickly as he had appeared.

What happened when I was five? Not that much I could remember. I read *The Jungle Books* for the first time but he didn't look like Mowgli; I got hit in the mouth with a seesaw but I don't think he was there...oh well.

17

So wouldn't that just figure, my guardian angel was a homosexual prostitute living on the streets of Manhattan. If I hadn't stopped to talk to him in the waiting room, my eyes would have never seen Larry off to the left, en route to the floor of the emergency room, throwing up with eyes rolling back into his head.

It couldn't be that simple, could it? I had seen him, I thought, a hundred times over the past ten years. But this time, it was really Larry. Down deep I knew it.

But my place was not to get too overly excited because I had been down this road before. I was always the one who had to be sensible in these situations.

At times it was a burden but at other times I was happy for my serenity. It was for others around me to get excited while I just wondered why I wasn't.

"Larry, Larry…it's Jamie," I said. I went by Jim now but my brother still remembered me by my nickname. No matter, he still didn't wake up.

I slapped him gently then hit him in the pit of his back like we used to do when he wouldn't shut up when we were kids. My brother Don and I would take turns so that Larry couldn't get out an intelligible word and finally give up on talking.

It worked, I got him up, yet he still had no idea who I was.

But I wasn't so sure he knew who he was either.

Chapter 3

Is he Larry or not:

"So you think he's your long lost brother?" the shrink said when we met in his office. "What makes you so sure if you haven't seen him in ten years?"

"Actually it's been thirteen years so I guess part of it is intuition," I answered. "But I do see a lot of the facial features and some of the mannerisms; here, look at this old picture."

Bellevue Hospital was an old institution well worn with the millions of patients seen there over the years. You could almost smell the indigents of the past covered up with the antiseptic hospital smell.

The doctor readjusted his glasses while examining the picture of Larry. I could see that he was overworked but dedicated.

"I do see some similarities between this shot and him and you. But I'm not ready to say that he is Larry Goodman. And neither is he."

"If you give me some access, I will know a lot more in a few days. Who else is there to help him through this time?"

"Just don't tell him that you think he's your brother."

***

"Who the hell are you? You're always hanging around my room," Larry said. "You enjoy watching people suffer or maybe you could score me a rock if you want to help out."

He threw up and pulled at his straps so he could scratch his face. This was a far cry from the innocent, almost-nerdy brother I had last seen at age thirteen in 1976

So, it turned out that Larry had a crack addiction as did many street people around the Tri-State area in the late eighties. He definitely wasn't enjoying the straps on his arms, with the DTs he was going through.

"I'm your br-no just someone who found you on the street. You reminded me of someone I used to know," I said. Telling Larry that I was his brother might be too much of a shock for his system which was just coming back into reality. Or so I thought.

"Get the fuck out of here," he said. "I don't need anyone's help except the man who brings me the rock."

"Well, you little shit; you needed someone's help last night when you almost died. You remember passing out in the emergency room?"

"Fuck no, you're full of shit."

"Well, you must have had a little too much crack cocaine and you tried to OD. But they saved your sorry ass."

"Saved me to entertain you?"

"I'm outta' here, see you later."

"Don't do me no fuckin' favors."

***

I saw the psychiatrist headed down the hallway.

"So, how much longer will he be in those straps and suffering with the DTs," I asked the doctor.

"It depends upon him. Could be a few more days, another week maybe," the shrink said. "Every case is different depending upon how long they've been addicted and their individual constitutions."

"Do you think it's a good idea for me to tell him I'm his brother yet?"

"Are you really sure that he is your brother? Sometimes we get our hopes up and develop a false confidence in things we want to believe."

"Even though he doesn't recognize me or even know who he is, I can tell from his mannerisms and the way he responded to something my brother Don used to do to him."

"I would wait…he's going through enough of a shock to his system now. What did you do that he seemed to respond to?"

I explained how we used to hit him in the back when we were in the back of the car to interrupt his speech.

"Oh, boys will be boys. I'm not sure that's a good barometer but let's see what develops in the next couple of weeks."

I could hear Larry retching yet again as Bellevue's automatic doors shut behind me. That reminded me of how hungry I was.

***

There's nothing like a slice or two of New York pizza when you haven't had some for a while. It wasn't just how it tasted but it was the whole ambiance of those smelly Manhattan streets bustling with millions of people on weekdays.

I grabbed a couple and a diet pop, and then headed down to the river to sit on a bench and clear my head. Although the open country, with its tall trees instead of skyscrapers, usually accomplished this best, there was something about seeing planes, trains and automobiles plus boats and bikes that helped me get centered.

I woke up a couple of hours later, barely remembering the pizza. I guess that I forgot I hadn't had any sleep. I had always thought that sleep was a waste of time but it definitely wasn't today.

If I was tired, I could fall asleep anywhere. Even on a bus to road basketball or baseball games while everyone else was getting psyched for the matchup.

My clearest thoughts were when I first woke up so I pondered upon the fact that we had all thought Larry might've jumped off a bridge on the opposite end of this island. Then I thought that I should call my brother Don and my father to let them know that I'd found Larry (my mother had passed away a few years earlier).

***

Sometimes it sucks being the sensible one who labors over every action to think every consequence through before taking said action. Of course, that was excepting the time I had slid bare ass down the moss-covered rocks to almost cut my foot off on the broken glass at the bottom. Thanks, Pickle (Mark Pascale) and Bruce for making enough room in the cooler for my foot! Maybe not only that time but other such times when I had to be the first to do something if dared.

***

A disheveled man approached and asked how I was doing; I knew what that meant.

Reaching into my pocket, I gave the panhandler a quarter as he came up to me. But then the thought got me. Who knew what other people I could meet from my past if the quarter hadn't been given. No, last night was enough of an adventure.

I reconsidered returning to the hospital but longed for a little fresh air away from Manhattan. Sometimes believing that I had moved back from New Mexico a couple of years ago, even if it was only a temporary move, was difficult.

Fresh air was much more of a commodity in the New York-New Jersey area and it took a little time out in the open to think out the yesterday's happenings.

Chapter 4

Remembrances:

"What are you going through Larry's old stuff for? Get out of there," my father yelled to me. He had set up a shrine in his home office to my youngest brother which, it was an unspoken rule, was never to be disturbed.

"I was just remembering our childhood a little," was my reply. "I'll put everything back."

I returned the high school football program, the ticket stubs and everything else to its original spot and pretended to put my youth behind me. I didn't know how to sneak stuff out to show to Larry to help him regain his identity. Maybe taking pictures of it was the way to go.

But I was a pretty darn good thief in my day. It had been a long time since I had stolen anything; with the fear of being pulled back into that life.

Thievery was kind of like doing drugs. It was too much fun. I realized at a pretty young age that if something was too much fun, there was always a payback.

Even like a hangover after you drank too much. So I learned to moderate. Of course that was made easier by the fact that my parents allowed me to do things moderately like smoke pot and drink when most of my friends did not.

Most people didn't believe that my parents let me get high. Once, before a Sha Na Na concert, I invited a group of people upstairs to my bedroom. My mother yelled up to open the windows and everyone knew we were allowed to light up.

Amy Wertheim and Amber still joke about shouting, "Thank you, Mrs. Goodman," as we departed.

I didn't try any hallucinogens until living in New Mexico around the age of twenty-one. They were so much fun that I was afraid to do them too often. About five or six experiments, mostly with mushrooms, maxed me out.

That was a lot less than most people I'd hung around with in high school and later on in life.

But obviously my youngest brother hadn't learned. Or maybe he just had an addictive personality I'd been lucky to have avoided.

When I moved back to the New York-New Jersey area, my father employed me part-time in the small advertising agency that he ran out of his house. Having written advertising copy for almost forty years, his ideas were starting to go stale.

"Did you hear me? Where have you been the last two days? I thought you were coming to work yesterday?" my father asked.

My mind had drifted but my father was usually able to get me back in focus at the office. Elsewhere, that was a different story since he still sometimes still treated me like I was a teenager.

He hadn't seen me much since my teen years, leading to conversations similar to this one we'd had when I was going out with some coworkers at my waiter job.

"You don't drink and drive, do you?" he'd asked.

"I haven't in a long time but I find it difficult to drive without drinking in New York area traffic," had been my response. He gradually stopped asking those kinds of questions.

My creative mind was full of unique ideas which he was able to polish so we made a pretty good team, most of the time. Luckily, I also cooked and waited tables at a mid-priced restaurant.

"I got called in to work at the Old Farmhouse," I told him. "We didn't have anything much going on here, so I helped out there."

My father wasn't ready to hear that I actually thought I had found Larry. After hiring a detective in the early 1980's and not ever wanting to move from the last place Larry had known he lived, Abraham Goodman had decided his youngest son was no longer alive.

"I left a message on your machine last night. Obviously you didn't play it back," my father said. "We got a rush job to do. If it works out, we could get a lot more work."

"I'm off for a couple of days now, so tell me what we need." I had heard about these rush jobs leading to more work before. When things were all said and done it was just that the client wanted things in a hurry.

Nonetheless, we brainstormed on his original idea to give it a little more pizzazz. The "Get Peanuts for Peanuts" campaign was under way with joyous elephants drowning in their favorite snack.

We got the preliminary work done and approved by the client. Then I had to deliver it to Madison Avenue the next day; I wouldn't be far from Bellevue so I would have my chance to check on Larry again.

Now if sneaking some memorabilia from the shrine was possible, maybe I could joggle Larry's burnt-out mind. Maybe Polaroids would be the best way to go but I would have to get my father out of the way with an afternoon nap; not a tough thing to do with him approaching seventy-three.

"Going to grab a bite? I think we got a lot done faster than we expected," I told him.

"I'll just stay in the office."

"Want me to make you a turkey sandwich? There's that good smoked turkey and Muenster to go with it."

"That sounds good."

He was almost snoring after the first bite as just the L-tryptophan's aroma seemed to put him under. I took my chances and snuck out with a handful of memorabilia from the shrine.

Chapter 5

Suspicions Unconfirmed:

My brakes screeched and brought my '82 Ford Econoline van to a stop on the Palisades Parkway as I approached Engelwood Cliffs. I had been looking at the pictures and other nostalgia while heading in my car towards Manhattan to kill two birds with one ten-dollar toll.

I didn't mind paying tolls too much, although there had never been any in New Mexico, as long as the roads are in good shape. But the George Washington Bridge and roads in Manhattan left a lot to be desired--when the asphalt wore out on the bridge, it was just replaced with sheets of metal which didn't offer a very smooth ride.

While anxiously waiting in line to pay the toll (there were also very rarely lines in New Mexico except at Taco Bell drive-ups), I looked at Larry's picture and tried to age it ten years. Just as I was sure that it was Larry in rehab, a slight difference in the nose was seen.

I flashed to Kevin Shaughnessy climbing the spans of the mighty bridge while we were in high school walking across the bridge. We'd walked the bridge to go to the city pretty often back then. Someday they'll probably charge a toll to do that.

But it was time to pay my ten bucks. My tires shook some metal and I was soon heading down the Franklin Delano Roosevelt Drive on the east side of Manhattan.

***

Finding street parking on 54th Street was unusual on a weekday and I quickly ran up the steps and dropped off the starter kit for the "Get Peanuts for Peanuts" program at 527 Madison.

I wasn't really thinking because my next stop was weighing heavily on my mind. What hint would be best to get Larry to remember who he was?

Or assure me that he actually was Larry? If only he would have recognized the VDB penny when mentioned to him, I could have been sure.

***

Then I saw it...a ticket stub from a football game between the New York Giants and the Pittsburgh Steelers. Now that was a game I really didn't care about who won.

But Larry would have cared.

***

So I found street parking near Bellevue. This was really my lucky day. Wondering how all the radio stations stayed in business with everybody's no radio signs in their windows. I made up one for my van.

***

Could this crack addict scam me if he wanted to? Maybe bringing my other brother with me next time would be a good idea.

"Looks like you're feeling a lot better today," I told Larry while walking into his room. "At least you're unstrapped."

This time his hands were over his face as he was trying to hold himself back from vomiting.

"Yeah, life's fuckin' grand," he said. "You get off on that sadistic shit watching me suffer, huh?"

"Really, it hurts me to watch you suffer. But I know you'll be better off in the long run."

"Why the hell do you care? You my friggin' guardian angel or something?"

At least he wasn't throwing anything at me. That would have been my other brother when he was younger. He was only half my size so

27

he'd usually pick up something, and often to throw it, to even things out.

But Don had mellowed considerably.

The water pitcher hit me in the head just as I was thinking how mellow Larry had been as a kid. Luckily, it was only a soft plastic on my hard head and it had emptied en route to its cranial collision.

Maybe my cranium was damaged previously to think that this was Larry.

Chapter 6

Childhood Memories:

The nurse came past just in time to see Larry pick up the pitcher off the floor.

"Everything alright in here?" she asked. She had probably heard my yell when I'd first been hit.

"Yeah, everything's fine," we responded in stereo like our parents had just caught us doing something wrong when we were little. My brother looked at me quizzically as the nurse shook her head and went about her rounds.

I think something finally began to click in Larry's head as it had been clicking in mine for the last few days. It might be time to look through the box of stuff I'd brought.

"Who's that bald guy? He looks sort of familiar," Larry said, pointing to a picture of my father from amongst the stuff I had brought from my dad's shrine.

"That's my father before he got a rug," I responded.

"Did he work for Mad Magazine…? He looks like one of the characters in there." He remembered that Mad was famous for using caricatures of their writers as characters in the magazine.

"No, but I know who you mean." I just hoped he didn't mean Alfred E. Newman, who didn't look anything like my father. "He was in advertising; went to college on the G.I. Bill when he still had a little hair after the war."

"Which war?"

"Here, let me show you," I said, rifling through the box for a picture of our father in uniform. "There it is."

I was glad that I'd brought a couple of old pictures of Dad. A half hour earlier, handing Larry the old picture under glass might not have been very smart but now I trusted that he wouldn't break it over my head.

"Ah, World War II, European Theater under Eisenhower," my brother said as quickly as I handed the picture to him. "Looks like he was stationed in London and Paris, medical corps."

"You know a little bit about the Big War, huh?" I was pretty convinced now that I had my brother sitting next to me.

"Yeah, remember learning about it in another life."

"Yeah, my parents got married when my father was shipping out in '42 and came back in '44. But they didn't have me, their first born, until '56."

"They sure waited a long time to have an asshole like you," he said with a laugh at the end.

"They still had two more assholes after that. Mom was forty-three when she had the last of us boys." I grabbed a family picture with me around age ten and Don about eight so Larry must have been around four.

"The two younger guys aren't bad looking but what happened to the older brother. You sure his father wasn't an escapee from the asylum?"

Every time Larry smiled, I thought that he looked more and more familiar. It was time to bring out the teenage pictures.

"See anything familiar about that guy?" I said while pointing to Larry around age thirteen in a picture of all three boys just before I'd headed west. The time had come to put my cards on the proverbial table.

"He's definitely more intelligent-looking than his older brothers."

Was he playing with me or not?

"Put the damned picture up next to your face and ask the nurse who it looks like."

"You think it looks like me! Is that why you keep hanging around here...you think I'm your brother or some shit?"

The water pitcher grew wings again and the feeling that things had been pushed too far sunk in just as the feeling of pain in my left ear did. Oh well, that just evened out with the pain in my right ear from my previous battle with the pitcher.

I didn't remember Larry being able to throw that accurately.

Matter of fact, he just wasn't as into sports as his two older brothers. All the more curious as to why he'd wanted to play football and why my parents had let him play when they wouldn't let me. The boy who'd studied up on WW II and collecting coins when I knew him returned his first kickoff for a touchdown in high school.

When the toothbrush got me in the eye, I knew it was time to head out. The football ticket slipped out of the box as I made a hasty retreat with him calling Ralph in the background.

Chapter 7

Take Me Out to the Rehab:

With my mind wandering even more than usual in admiration of the Gothic architecture with its gargoyle rainspouts, I tripped on my way down the steps outside of Bellevue. Luckily, I caught myself on the railing but not before losing my marbles on the marble post, leaving me a little dazed.

I dropped my boxful of mementos and, before I could find what had leaked out of my skull, someone picked up something shiny. They ran down the street with someone chasing them.

"Get away from me…we all gots to make a living!" I heard someone yell. I could see one person dragging another back towards me.

"You're still visiting that street rat, huh? Guess you don't mind the smell of the DTs?" My rescuer from the other night seemed to show up at the hospital, or wherever, at the most opportune times.

Still coming to, I was a little more confused as to who he was, holding a page of proof pennies. "Where'd you come from again?"

"Just passing by, trying to get into trouble," he said. "And keep you out of trouble. Recognize him?"

It was Ronnie,er, Veronica again. She sheepishly handed me back the coins.

"This can't be real; you all filming a TV show or something? Seems like you, Ronnie, are always getting me in trouble and you are always passin' by when I'm in trouble."

"Just cruising for trannies or someone else I can have some fun with. I sense some cops coming. I'm out of here." He dropped Ronnie and she ran off but I noticed a plastic shopping bag on the sidewalk behind the marble base.

."Hey, you dropped this," I yelled but he was already gone around the pretzel cart on the corner.

I was still a little slow after banging my head. Ronnie took off down the street and disappeared just as the cops pulled up. I opened the bag up and what I saw made me think I was in some fantasy world. A 1979 Super Bowl program and ticket stub for the Steeler- Cowboy championship game in Miami.

"You okay there?" a cop yelled from the car.

"Yeah, just fell but I'm alright."

"Don't need an ambulance or a ride to the hospital?"

"Naah, I'll be okay in a minute or two. Thanks."

***

"Hey, Don, whatcha' up to?" A typical start to what could be an atypical conversation between the two older Goodman brothers.

"Just practicing a little." My brother Don had become pretty accomplished on the guitar, a lot of it due to playing until his fingertips had bled while cutting high school.

Approaching Don on the subject of Larry was not an easy thing to do. He lived through that whole tragic time with my family while I had been 2,000 miles away and he pretty much thought that Larry had killed himself.

Just seeing the diary where Larry talked about that was different than talking to Larry when he'd been fifteen like Don had the chance to. So I had to lure Don into the city and then find a reason to sidetrack him to Bellevue.

"I got free Met tickets for Thursday afternoon. You don't have to work, do ya?"

33

"Why in the hell would you want to go to a Met game?"

"So I can find more reasons why the Yankees are better and collect other ways to pick on the Queens of Queens. And I did get the tickets for free. It's Woody Harrelson Day; they'd have to give those tickets away for anyone to show up."

"Hey now, that's Buddy. Not Woody." Don always liked the opposite team than I did and Harrelson had been his favorite player when we were growing up. I think part of that was because we had the same birthday.

"What's the difference? One can't catch a break on Cheers and the other can't catch a baseball."

"Yeah, yeah, yeah. So you should just give me the tickets and I'll take Andrew." Andrew was Don's five-year-old.

"I thought maybe we could hit a jazz club afterwards. I know you always like to sit in if possible."

"I guess that would be cool if you don't wear your Yankee cap."

"Pick you up around noon Thursday then, cool?"

"Later."

***

"Remind you of anything," I asked while showing Don the program.

"Yeah, it's a Super Bowl XIII program, where'd you get that. A yard sale or something?" Don knew about my penchant for second-hand stuff.

"You wouldn't believe it if I told you; you do know what year Super Bowl XIII was played, right? Look at the bottom."

"Oh, 1979. That would have been the game Larry said he was going to. What are you thinking you might have found him again?" Don had lost patience with me as I had "found" Larry several times before only to unfind him.

So I told Don the story about the near-mugging, Veronica, my guardian angel and the crack addict.

"It does sound strange but which one do you think is Larry?"

"The crack addict. He's going through DTs at Bellevue."

"So that's what your plan was, to get me out here and to make a short side trip to go visit this druggie who you think is Larry. Do you even have tickets to the Mets?"

"Would I lie to you?"

"Yes." My brother knew me too well.

"You're absolutely correct but I'm not lying this time. I do have the tickets but I was figuring to go by the hospital after the game and before the jazz clubs start hopping."

"Let me think about it," Don said as we got to the bridge.

Chapter 8

Don 1, Jim 0:

"Now, that's where the real hitters hit, runners run and World Series are won," I said to Don as we passed 161st Street and Yankee Stadium across the East River. He didn't even have to look up to know what I was alluding to.

"The Mets just won in '86. When was the last time the Yankees won?"

"When was the last time the Mets won two in a row? And I don't mean getting the top draft pick two years in a row." I wasn't about to kiss his ass just so he would go with me to Bellevue.

Ah, sibling rivalry, it's a wonderful thing. I still remember the time I was running the football when Don had jumped on my back since he couldn't get me off my feet and told me he would punch me "in the balls" if I didn't pretend like he'd tackled me.

"Let's just get there; maybe I'll get to see my favorite shortstop on the way in to Shea (Stadium)."

I couldn't let him get the last word in. Well, I guess sticking my index finger in my mouth and pretending to throw up was an action, not a word.

***

As we waited to get over the toll-free Brooklyn Bridge, there was a backup. There's always a backup where there's no toll and, as previously mentioned, there's always a backup at the toll booths. So basically, bridge traffic in New York City is always constipated as the Mets are in getting runners across home plate.

"Clean your windshield?" I barely heard through my window left slightly open. The potential cleaner or soiler as the case usually was since they used dirty water and an oily rag, approached me from behind the driver's side.

"Go ahead," I said, pushing a dollar bill through the window.

My George Washington disappeared as quickly as its new owner.

"Guess I just helped someone to buy another bottle of cheap wine. Just as well," I commented.

"You probably wouldn't have been able to see out of it after they were done anyway."

I moved a total of five feet in the next few minutes.

"Jim…Jim," a shadowy figure was yelling and waving some money in the air. It's amazing how some people can have a dark aura even in the daytime.

"I don't believe this shit. You won't believe who that is, Don."

"It's Larry, right?"

"Not quite…it's the guy who saved me from being mugged."

"Whaattt. That's friggin weird."

"Here's the money that tranny tried to rip you off for. Bitch should know she can't get away with nothin' while I'm around," my savior said.

"Who in the hell are you? What's your name? Why do you keep showing up all the time?"

"Cops are around…gotta' go. But I'm Benjamin, later." And he was gone as quickly as he'd shown up.

"Strange shit, huh?" I said to Don.

"If you deserved one, I would say that dude was your guardian angel."

* * *

Shea Stadium didn't have the long-steeped tradition of Yankee Stadium but it did have a character of its own. It had started out with

37

the Amazin' Mets in 1962, who were clowns until they got some pitching and won the '69 World Series.

I didn't want Don to know but I was actually hoping the Mets would win so he would feel like going to the rehab. We had seen Bud Harrelson on his way in but only from the back. Plus he was surrounded by autograph hounds.

Luckily, the Mets eked out a 4-3 win over the Houston Astros with Dwight Gooden getting the W. Darryl Strawberry, who'd had a lot of problems with his teammates that season, knocked in the winning run in the eighth inning.

We waited for Harrelson to exit the stadium but no such luck finding him. After a couple of early hot dogs and more than a few beers to wash them down, we decided to get some real food at Joe's Clam Bar on the water in Brooklyn.

Sheepshead Bay, like many neighborhoods in Brooklyn, wasn't what it used to be before the days of urban renewal. But Joe's was still every bit as good as I could remember it. From the fresh clams on the half shell to the calamari, scungilli and fresh Italian bread.

And the beer wasn't bad either. In fact, it was so good we stayed for a few rounds after a couple of glasses of Chianti with dinner.

"Shit, it's eight o'clock. Visiting hours are over," I said to Don.

"So, I guess we can't go to the hospital anyway. Bummer."

"Yeah, I know you really were looking forward to going, huh? Still want to catch a set or two on the way home?"

"That was the original plan. I'm tired of the same old places, though. Let's check out the Village for anything new."

"Sure, but this time let's make sure it's a jazz club… before we park and see that it's really a gay bar."

"Okay, I'll see if I can find a gay jazz bar. We'll just pretend we're a couple. Nobody ever believes we're brothers anyway."

"That would definitely be a new experience."

"About as new as us actually acting like brothers."

Chapter 9

One of Those Nights:

"LGBT? I wonder if that means large breasts or large butts. It says jazz on the sign, too. Could be an interesting combination," I told Don about the place just off of Christopher St. in Greenwich Village.

"A little more interesting than you might think," Don said. He seemed to know what actually might be happening behind those doors.

It's not that I had never been to that part of the Village before but my time in New Mexico hadn't exposed me to that acronym just yet. The bar's patrons would expose themselves to me before the night was over.

"The music sounds alright," I remarked after parking the car. "There's a little syncopation going on in there."

"I'm sure that syncopation and improvisation are going full force on stage and in the alley."

The doorman was bouncing to the music, looking sort of like a seventies David Bowie on steroids, and Don handed him a twenty.

When I walked in, I wasn't sure whether the spectacle or the music hit my senses first. While the stage was decorated quite colorfully for the Dyke Ellington Orchestra, the vocalist was dressed as flamboyantly as her voice was sultry.

"I don't think I've seen a jazz club with this loud of a color scheme before," I said to Don with surprise. "And they misspelled Duke...or is that on purpose?"

"You have been in New Mexico too long. Of course it's on purpose...Bi-Lee Holiday is the vocalist."

"Only in New York. In some ways I miss shit like this and in others I'm happy for the things I get out West that I could never get here."

"Yeah, but you still can't get the culture that you can get here."

"That's why you're moving to Vermont?"

"Plenty of jazz there, too. But maybe not like this."

Just as he said that, a feather boa Holiday had been wearing came flying across our table with several patrons flying behind it. One made it look like he...or she was attempting to grab it when they actually grabbed my dick.

"Oops, sorry," the offender said without looking up.

"No, you're not," I said. "But I guess that was part of the cover charge."

"You're here, you're queer, you should have no fear," the groper said. "Or did you think that LGBT meant large breasts?"

The tranny looked up and it was Veronica...er, Ronnie. I checked my wallet which, of course, was missing.

"I thought that grab felt familiar. What the hell are you doing here?" I yelled. "Give me back my damn wallet."

The bouncer was on his way over to the table and I could see that it was Benjamin as he appeared out of the smoke.

"Ronnie, get the hell away from him before I kick you out."

"But they're straight...what the fuck are they doing here?"

"Wallet," Benjamin wasn't backing down. "And that wasn't just a request."

He gave the wallet back, not unrelentingly. I checked and my money plus ID was still there.

Don seemed pretty amazed by the whole scene. I would have concurred had these people not already met up with me a few times.

Veronica reached for the feather boa which had landed in front of Don. She couldn't quite grab the end of it.

"Can I stay and talk to you for a minute, Jim?" Veronica asked. "I won't try to steal anything from you or your friend."

"I'll kick his ass out right now," Benjamin said.

"No, it's alright." I said. "Wouldn't mind getting some answers myself and by the way you don't remember my brother Don?"

"Just don't buy him a drink. It will fuck with his hormones," Benjamin said.

"Yeah, about those hormones...no, that's your business, Veronica," I said. "But why are you living on the street and just trying to scam and steal your way through life?"

"I don't have to listen to this shit!"

She went to go storm off while Don pretended to just be listening to the music. The feather boa was still on the table in front of him when Benjamin came back over.

"Mind if I sit down for a minute?"

"No problem, Benny. It's the least I could do after all you've done for me the last few days. But, tell me, who are you?"

"I told you that I was Benjamin, don't call me fuckin' Benny! Now let me tell you about Ronnie. Apparently, she went out with this guy a few years ago and he broke her heart when he moved 2,000 miles away. She started to realize more and more that maybe men weren't for her and began hormone therapy."

"That sounds like you, Jim," Don said. "You can really pick 'em."

"So anyway, she was finally ready for the operation but was running low on money since no insurance would cover it," Benjamin continued. "She went to some place in southern Colorado where a doctor had performed hundreds of these operations successfully and more economically than in New York.

But, as luck would have it, she ran into that same ex in, I believe it was Raton, New Mexico. It was so upsetting to her that she had to come back to the only area she knew anyone."

41

"Oh, she probably went to Trinidad for the sex change and Raton was right over the pass," I said. This set my mind thinking even more that I was the ex who'd made her realize her true identity.

"Yeah, she said he was camping or something."

Sugarite Canyon is a beautiful state park which straddled the Colorado-New Mexico border just outside Raton. It was one of my favorite places especially when the leaves were changing.

"Anyways, her money ran out and her family and friends had given up on her so she had to find a way to continue her hormones."

Some straight people had started some trouble at the door and when Benjamin heard the ruckus, he headed over there to back up the doorman along with several other employees.

"Gotta say that this has been one mysterious night," Don said, adding that we should probably leave once the excitement at the door was finished. He was pretty drunk but I had stopped after the two-drink minimum since I was driving.

Chapter 10

One of Those Nights - Part 2:

"We should sneak into the hospital tonight," I said as we were on our way back uptown. I had never snuck into anything besides peep shows in the city and maybe a concert or two but definitely more peep shows. But getting in backstage to the Telluride Jazz and Bluegrass festivals and making people think that I was a roadie was something I'd only been able to accomplish out West,

"So, I know I lived near you in New Mexico for like a year but that was with Liz," Don said. "But I never asked you what the whole story was why you moved there...was it because of your problems with Mom?"

"Sort of...when Mom took me to court for assault, it made me realize that I'd never really felt at home in Jersey, Long island or even White Plains. When I first got to New Mexico, I felt more at home there than I ever had in my whole life.

Even though people were speaking Spanish to me and I didn't know a lick of it."

"What really did happen between you and Mom? I only heard her side and I've come to realize that she had her problems then."

"Well, I was living in Ramsey workin' for the veterinarian but was at the Hillsdale house waiting for you guys to get home from school, if you weren't cutting that day, when my eyes closed while watching TV.

Mom got home before anyone else and it was raining so she was honking for someone to open the garage door.

I didn't come quickly enough and she started yelling and pulled my hair. I knocked her arm off and she fell, apparently bruising her hip. I got out of there and didn't come back for a few weeks.

"Wait, let me go back to the months before that when I was trying to get Mom some help. I tried first to get her to see a rabbi, then a counselor, a shrink and finally, even a priest that Pickle helped me line up,"

"So that probably antagonized her a little to start with?" Don asked.

"Yeah, I'm sure it did but she needed some help and there were concerns about you and Larry as well as her. So, when I returned the next time, more or less the same thing happened except for Mom pulled a knife on me.

"I managed to grab it out of her hand but she was pissed so she went to the police station and filed charges. I was arrested but released on my own recognizance and didn't come around the house any more.

"I thought the better of filing charges against her and when the case made it to court, Mom said she would drop all charges if her eldest son didn't come around again. I agreed, stating emphatically that she would never have to worry about that.

"She said that you were eating our food when you came over and that was another problem?" Don said.

"Yeah, but I was bringing food, mostly shoplifted, every time I passed by. Even after the court agreement, food was dropped off...sometimes by my friends when it was too close to the time Mom got out of work."

"So that guy Jack was the one who made you decide on New Mexico? You only saw Mom when it was time to get your Bar Mitzvah savings bonds after that and the time you picked Larry up right before you left, huh?" Don looked outside and heaved a sigh of relief.

"Yeah. Unfortunately I talked to her one more time when she accused me of hiding Larry from her in New Mexico. My reaction was not good since I told her that as much as I hated her, I would never hide her son from her. I told her 'fuck you' and slammed the phone down.

"But, yeah, it was Jack and his family who made me decide to go west. Rudy and Dotty Dautel...Jack's parents... were some great people who came into my life at a time when I needed them. I was having dinner at their house every Sunday when I was driving the ice cream truck and they could tell that I needed to get out of New Jersey.

I found out that Jack and his whole family had some relatives in Albuquerque and were moving west in 1977. So I split in '76 after the ice cream season was over and got to New Mexico before them. I got into the snack wagon business and Jack started in it when he came a few months later."

"Didn't you have a problem with some girl, too, before you left?" Don asked.

"Yeah, remember when you guys moved out of the Hillsdale house and I took our dog Peppy. Well, I had quit the veterinarian and moved to a house in Westwood with six other guys. Well, that didn't work out. No surprise there but I moved in with Laurie in Allendale above the cleaners.

"Peppy never liked her and I found out why. She would steal money while I was driving the ice cream truck everyday. I would let the dog out on the roof in the morning and she would close the window so he couldn't get back in. and steal whatever loose change or ones I had laying around."

"And you still don't pick up your loose change."

"Yeah, never learned that but I did learn to trust dogs more than people."

I noticed the sign to get onto the bridge and saw a smile from Don. His distraction had worked so now I had to figure out another way to get him into the city to meet Larry.

Chapter 11

Larry Gets a Visitor:

"Don't read any more into this than what it is," Don said as he entered Larry's room at Bellevue.

I had wracked my brain for a couple of days as to how to get Don to come and verify Larry's identity. I guess the Vulcan Mind Meld used on Don had worked.

"They told you the rules up front, right? He's still going through some DTs," I said.

"Yeah, yeah, I've had enough friends in rehab. I know the rules."

"So, who is this? He don't look like you, thank god, so he can't be your brother. And he's skinny, too," Larry said.

"Yeah, and he's got a bigger nose, too. My little brother didn't always eat his food growing up and I ate his," I said.

"Now you brought your brother here so he could try and convince me that I'm your long- lost younger brother. Well, it ain't gonna' work."

"Let's get this shit straight. I don't believe you're Larry. But I was in the city and I figured Jim would buy me lunch if I showed up here," Don said.

"Yeah, maybe a liquid lunch at McSorley's along with some Sabretts," I said. "Anyway, Larry and I were just talking about this football ticket I dropped after he bopped me with a water pitcher last time I was here."

"Water pitcher…ha, that sounds like something I would have done when I was younger. Remember the flying pizza and the fork to eat it with?" Don said.

"Yeah, that was the first time I babysat for my little bros. I brought the pie back from Necroto's in Massapequa on my bike but my brother wasn't really wanting to listen to me."

"Yup, pretty cool when the fork stuck in your chest," Don said. "Remember, you thought you were gonna' die?"

"What the fuck, you trying to jog my memory or what. Well…this shit ain't working. But I do remember something about this football game," Larry said.

"Huh, you remember going with Dad?" I said anxiously. "You finally starting to remember some of your past?"

"Yeah… I am…it's kind of foggy. But, oh yeah, I remember that you were always a fuckin' asshole," Larry said.

Don laughed and said, "Maybe he is Larry."

"So what about the Jets-Steelers game? Where did you sit?"

"Oh, I wasn't at the game that I can remember. Just remember the Jets getting their asses kicked once again and Mean Joe Greene knocking that pussy Joe Namath out of the game."

Larry knew that I was a Jet fan and that Namath had been my favorite player since meeting him and getting his autograph at the car show in the N.Y. Coliseum around '65 or '66. But I may have let that slip during my last visit.

"Yeah, Namath was a pussy, wasn't he?" Don said. "Every time somebody touched him, the little baby got hurt."

"Right, sure…but he could still throw a football like nobody else. So you sure you didn't go to that game?"

"If I went, I think I'd remember it," Larry said. "It's not like my childhood was full of great memories."

"Where'd you grow up?" I asked. "What do you remember?"

"Well, I don't remember much but I did hear that I fell on my head a couple of times. When I was an infant, I fell out of the fuckin 'car 'cause I wasn't buckled in and that got that series of events started. Maybe that's why I don't remember much."

"See, Don, don't you remember that happening to Larry? Remember he fell out of the car in Massapequa?"

"Yeah, I suppose," Don said. "That probably happened to thousands of kids every year, though."

"My parents were always yelling at each other or at one of us kids. But they didn't fuckin' cuss, I learned that on my own."

"You don't remember anything about your house or the area it was in or your brothers or parents other than they fought a lot?" I said.

"I do remember my oldest brother as an asshole, another brother not as much of an asshole but they used to hit me when they thought I talked too much. I tried not to sit in the middle of the car's back seat because that way they couldn't fuckin' team up on me."

"But they wouldn't let you sit on the end 'cause they were afraid you'd fall out of the car again," Don said. "At least he got the part right about the oldest brother being an asshole."

Chapter 12

Pizza, Hot Dogs or Beer-All Three:

"So, where you wanna' go for late lunch. It's almost happy hour?" I said to Don as we walked out of Bellevue.

"You don't gotta' buy me lunch, it's no biggie. Let's get a Sabrett while we think about it," Don said after spying a nearby hot dog cart.

He knew that offer would never be turned down. When I'd worked as a messenger in Manhattan during my summers while in school, I made the Sabrett hot dogs a staple of my diet. They were the quickest way to grab some nutrition on my way to the Times Square peep shows where I spent the duration of my lunch hours.

"Kraut, onions and mustard," I told the vendor.

"Git da mustard ova dere!!" he told me in a thick accent. I must have forgotten where I was and thought that customer service might be part of the equation. I offered up my money.

"Already paid, dat woman ova dere," he pointed to…, uh, Veronica, er…Ronnie. "She paid for bot dogs."

"What the hell…what are you doing here?" I said to Ronnie while staring at Don. "You recognize her, right?"

Don said he did recognize her but still seemed wary.

"C'mon over here," Ronnie said, waving to me. He hadn't totally gained my trust just by buying hot dogs.

Holding tightly onto my wallet, I made my way over. "I'm trying to make up for some of my past misdeeds," he said.

49

"Why the sudden change of heart?" I could see a different aura surrounding Ronnie.

"I had this dream a couple of nights ago and it totally changed me. I thought I saw God and he said..."

I couldn't help myself. "Wait...you looked pretty changed to me a couple of weeks ago compared to the last time I saw you. How could you make any more drastic changes than that?"

"Jiiiimmmm...let him talk," Don said.

"Yeah, you can make a joke out of anything? I think that's the reason we broke up to begin with."

"Obviously, you were looking for something a little different in a man. Just look at yourself. But anyway, go on."

"Well, yeah, so God told me that there were much better things in my future if I would quit going down the wrong path. Shoplifting and stealing from people just isn't the way for me to go, he said."

I knew what was coming next. "And you were standing on a ladder which went infinitely into the heavens while he was talking to you?" I asked.

"Yeah, how'd you know?"

"Cause that's the same fuckin' story I told you that happened to me when I was nineteen. You're so full of shit." I walked off, "Thanks for the hot dogs anyways."

"But...but, that's what..." Ronnie said.

"Well, at least he didn't try to steal anything from you this time." Don said.

"I suppose, something did seem a little different. I guess without him stealing anything, Benjamin didn't have to show up either."

***

"Well, I guess after taking the bus into the city, you knew you could at least get a ride home from me," I said to Don. Vehicles were inconvenient in Manhattan but I still felt stranded without mine.

"Yeah, you don't have to take me home but it would make things easier. What about lunch?"

"McSorley's for a liquid lunch? Or there's a good pizza place around the corner?"

The oldest constantly open tavern in the country was always a good place to get an idea. If you get there before the stock markets close, it's not too crowded.

"It'll be tough to beat all those Wall Street preppies over there but we can try to get a couple of brews." Literally, you had to have a couple there because you had to order two at a time and they only had light and dark of their original home brews. But they're small and nobody went over there for just two.

When properly motivated, I could weave my way through city traffic like a cabbie. I was deciding on light or dark beer when we passed Giuseppi's Pizza. The decision had been made.

"So I guess it's beer first, pizza later?" Don said. "Hey, there's a spot and it's 2:35."

"We should be able to get seats... now, that's exciting."

* * *

You can't go for just one beer at McSorley's but they're small and they had perfected the recipe after being open since 1854.

"You know, whether that's Larry or not, I feel some sort of bond with him. You've got a lot of weird shit happening on all ends to really make a rational decision...what, with Ronnie and Benjamin and all," Don said.

"I don't know how but somehow it's all related. Sometimes I'm sure that he's Larry and other times not so sure."

"While there are some strange coincidences, I think they're just that. Coincidences...crazier shit happens in the city every minute."

"Yeah, like now." I pointed to Ronnie sitting down. I called the waiter over and said, "Don't let that dude who just came in buy my beer; in fact, can I get my ticket now?"

"He already did that before he even sat down."

"Son of a bitch, he goes from a thief last week to a stalker this week."

My transmission slipped as the van peeled out while we headed home. The road was a little wet so I thought nothing of it.

"The hell with the pizza, we're outta here. We can eat in Jersey."

Chapter 13

Transmission Problems:

I wasn't sure when getting back to Manhattan would be possible. Besides Veronica/Ronnie seeming to be everywhere I went, making up some hours at work was a necessity. And maybe it was better for Larry to get a little more on the ball and off the 8-ball.

But the van had other ideas. As I headed to the Old Farmhouse Restaurant to pick up some hours, the transmission seemed to have a few more issues.

The road to the restaurant had some spots with a shoulder and some without. Luckily the van broke down at one with room on the roadside. A tow truck came to pick the van up about a half-mile from work but I was already too late and they had already filled my shift.

"Is it okay if I ride with you to the closest transmission place?" I asked the driver.

"Yeah, sure. I'll take you to B & R Trannies, a new place almost to the Jersey border on 303. It comes highly recommended."

"Thanks, uh…what's your name? I'm Jim."

"What's today, Thursday…yeah, I'm Steve. Depends on the day of the week as to which cops are working, he, he."

"I can relate to that. Good to meet you, Steve."

"Hop on in."

"So, these guys just opened here but people are speaking highly of them already, huh?"

"Yeah, I guess they had a shop near the GW Bridge in Jersey and a lot of people used them over the years. So they're not totally new to the area."

"I never thought my tranny would go out on this van…it just seemed to go all of the sudden. Even after all the preventive maintenance over the years."

"Well, you just never know. Here we are."

The caricatures in the logo looked vaguely familiar but it was difficult to place them with their exaggerated features.

"Who are the owners…I sort of recognize them from somewhere?"

"I know one of them is Benjamin and I'm not sure about the other. Just don't call Benjamin Benny!"

"Ooohhh shit. No, it can't be. There's lots of Benjamins who don't like to be called Benny," I was thinking out loud. "His partner's not a weird-looking guy named Ronnie, is…"

Just then, a greasy hand tapped me on the shoulder. "Tranny problems, Jim?" I'd recognize that voice anywhere.

"In more ways than one, Ver…er, Ronnie. Steve, can we take the van somewhere else?" I started to get back into the tow truck.

"What, do you guys know each other? This really is the best place around. I'd have to charge you to go another twenty miles to a shop not as good as this one."

Benjamin came over to see what the fuss was about. "Hey Jim, long time no see."

"Not long enough for me not to see Ronnie. I don't feel good letting him work on my van."

"I'll oversee everything personally. We really are good at what we do. Ronnie just has his moments when he slips every once in a while."

"Yeah, I know you've been watching over me like a guardian angel the past few weeks. How come you only like to be called Benjamin?"

"You can call me Binyamin but it confuses people when they see B & R. Binyamin means Benjamin in—"

"Hebrew. Yeah, that was my great grandfather's name. I never met him, he died in the late 1930s." I had never met either of my great grandfathers and it had been a long time since I'd thought of my dad's grandfather who'd been a carpenter. He got run over by a Model A. Two of them actually, and the front of the transmission on the second one had hit him in the head when he'd tried to get back up.

"Yeah, that was the first Ford with a tranny as a separate component. That hurt…er, I mean that probably would have hurt. A little different than your Ford to say the least."

"Just trust us, Jim," said Veronica. "We do the best work for the best price, especially for you."

"Alright, lemme just make sure there's no loose change layin' around and don't clean the windows!"

Chapter 14

Breaking in the Tranny:

Benjamin called two days later to tell me that my van was ready and the transmission was shifting "smooth as silk." But his voice sounded a little different. Perhaps I was just uneasy. I had to work at my father's office soon but decided that getting the van was more important.

I didn't want to leave it near Ronnie any longer than I had to in case she…he had another setback. So I called Don and he was on his way to an out-of-town gig. My sister Margie, technically my stepsister but it's really more about feelings than blood, offered to take me and my other sister Meri went along.

"Need some gas money or anything, Marge?" I said as we left the house. I hadn't told them yet about Larry since I thought they might get overly excited. I wanted to be sure.

"No, Jim, I'm good."

"You didn't ask me," Meri stated as she searched the radio for the perfect song.

"Merrrriiii!" Margie yelled and her younger sister knew what she meant.

"You know that I would always buy you anything you wanted when you're with me, Meri," I said.

"I'm sorry…I didn't…," Meri started to say.

"Don't be sorry, just remember that you're never left out when you're with me," I said.

We stopped to get a couple of Diet Cokes plus a bag of Fritos and soon were at the transmission shop.

"Jim, that guy looks like familiar. He looks a little like your father. I've seen him somewhere," Margie said. "What do you guys think?"

Benjamin was approaching the car and, although he was still recognizable, his looks had changed. And his voice cracked a little.

"Some friends of yours, Jim? Nice looking girls."

"These are my sisters. Margie driving and Meri sitting shotgun. This is Benjamin."

"I didn't know you had sisters…they know what you've been up to lately?"

***

If Larry would have still been around, our melded families would have been like *The Brady Bunch* ten years apart when my dad had remarried. I was ten years older than the eldest girl, Melissa; Don a decade older than Margie and Larry about the same separation from Meri. Of course, my father's offspring were already living on their own while the girls were finishing school.

Meri was still in middle school when Susan Schorr had married Allan Goodman. So I actually gotten to watch her grow through the awkward teen years and was more of an older brother to her than her sisters. I'd helped her with everything from giving chopsticks lessons to her classmates to passing her driving test.

And it wasn't just one way, Meri was the little sister I never had. She made me smile every time I saw her and, years later, even Susan would say that we had a strange sort of connection more so than her other sisters had with me.

***

"No, they don't know who I've met lately, some things are better left hush-hush."

I don't think either girl was paying attention to what we were saying as much as they were looking at Benjamin. Their wheels were turning.

"What's your last name, Benjamin?" Margie asked.

"Yeah, you and Jim look like you could be related," Meri added.

"I assure you that we're not related," Benjamin said. "My last name is Epstein."

"Epstein…huh?? I know some Epsteins…yeah, in New Mexico." I lied and abruptly stopped without wanting to cause any more speculation. I was also surprised that he had volunteered his last name so easily.

"Who knows, somewhere way back we could be related," Benjamin's voice cracked until by the end of the sentence, he was almost inaudible.

"What's wrong with your voice and you seem to be changing physically, too?" I asked.

"Male menopause, I guess."

"Where's Ronnie, anyway? I never seen you without seeing him at the same time."

"Oh, yeah, he kinda wore himself out workin' on yer van. Hey, I got other customers…let's get your van. Good to meet you, girls."

I could see that both Margie and Meri looked puzzled. "Thanks for the ride, Marge. Catch you later."

As I walked in to the office, I noticed Benjamin began walking differently, slightly effeminate.

Chapter 15

My Fairy Godfather:

"He's gone," the nurse said. "We couldn't hold him here when he wanted to leave. Most likely he's trying to score again."

"Shit, god damn it. I should have come back sooner. But I wanted to give him some time," I said, having finally returned to Bellevue. "Did he leave any address?"

"Yeah, sure. The street."

"Well, I guess that's where I'm headed. Can I use yer phone?"

"Sure, go ahead."

Don's machine picked up. "Hey Don, he's fuckin' gone again. Larry took off from the hospital, I'll call you later."

***

"I thought I found him but now I lost him again," I told Sergeant Fairgate.

"Amazing after all this time. Where was he at?"

"Bellevue, found him OD'd in the E.R. Got him to check in to rehab about two weeks ago. But he left yesterday...damn. Hope he didn't feel abandoned cause I wanted to give him some time to absorb what I'd been telling him. Seemed like he was coming around...damn." I handed him a recent picture.

He studied the picture intently. "He looks sort of familiar; probably bounced through here a couple of times. Let me make a copy."

"He was recovering from crack; he seemed to be on his way."

"Yeah, horrible stuff, that. Lemme see what I can do and keep me informed if you find him. Jest don't raid no crack houses without backup, huh?"

"I won't, but you know it just sucks when you're so close. Thanks."

***

I started looking near Bellevue and decided I'd work in ever-widening circles until I found Larry. Putting up missing posters in Manhattan seemed like a worthless cause since you could see handbills of all kinds posted everywhere, most of which ended up as part of the sidewalk.

But I had made some copies of Larry's picture and thought it was worth showing around. I went to hand the picture to two cops.

"Already got it; Missing Persons gave us dis oilier."

"Ah, Fairgate's no bull shitter. Thanks."

"He's your long lost brudder, huh?"

"Yeah, maybe. I wasn't a hundred per cent sure yet."

"Good luck, Mac."

I worked my way around the burnt out block and showed the picture to a woman of the night whose eyes were just adjusting to the daylight.

"You ain't de only mudder fucker lookin' for his ass. He owe some money to some people, da wrong people. How much he owe you?"

"Nothing, if anything, I might owe him. He might be my brother. I'll be around looking for him. There's a couple of bucks in it for you if you can help me find him."

"Hope you find him before Luther do. He don't seem like a bad boy."

"Yeah, I hope so too."

So I continued down the street, stepping over needles and other small drug paraphernalia, and, no surprise, there was a crime scene. The whole neighborhood usually came out to see who'd died, I think, to figure out how to steal their stuff.

60

"Luther...oh, Luther," a woman's voice yelled out. There were probably a few Luthers in this area but maybe he was the one Larry owed money to.

"Guess I'm off the hook, dude. This is the closest I been to Luther since he fronted me dat shit six months ago," the street urchin next to me said.

Maybe it was the same Luther...guess I could find Larry before Luther could. I showed the other crackhead my brother's picture.

"Yeah, know him. Pretty cool dude; haven't seen him for a couple of weeks."

"I think he's my younger brother who disappeared ten years ago." I decided to go to the copy shop and make some copies of my phone number. But I gave him a handwritten copy. "There's a few bucks in it if you help me find him."

I saw the clock on the wall of the copy shop and realized I had to wait tables in an hour and a half. I wanted to search more for Larry but I had to make sure not to lose my job in the meantime. Maybe Don would come back with me in a day or two.

The changing voice of a prepubescent boy rang out from behind me. "Jim...Jim!"

It was hitting twilight and I couldn't see any tween age boys nearby. Out of the shadows, a figure emerged and I wasn't too sure.

"Jim...Jim. It's me, Benjamin." I was able to see him a little better.

"Boy, I am grateful for your help but you look like shit and what the hell happened to your voice?"

"How vould you look at over a hundred years old? It's a good thing my family left before the Bolsheviks came."

"Bolsheviks? A hundred? Binyamin Epstein? What the hell? How you workin' on transmissions? Naomi Epstein. She mean anything to you?"

"One question at a time Yeah, as you suspected, your grandmother Naomi was my daughter. Having sex with trannies is..."

I wouldn't let him finish. "So how long you been watching over me?"

"Just a few weeks full time since you started your last search for Larry."

"And sex with trannies? Wait, so what were you doing before that?"

"Watching over Larry for the last decade; he's quite a handful. But do you remember almost drowning when you were five?"

"You," I said, pointing at him.

"And when Don was lost overnight on that campout in Harriman State Park?"

"Okay, okay. So where's Larry now?"

"Dunno, gotta go."

"Hey…wait."

It was no use; he was gone. Looking for trannies or working on them, guess that was where he was probably off to.

Chapter 16

Fantasy or Reality:

"Oh, hey Don, you won't believe this." My brother had called me back.

"What, you found Larry again and he had the birthmark so you're sure it's him now?"

"No, you'll never get this in twenty questions. Benjamin, his last name is Epstein, is not just my guardian angel. He was our great grandfather and now is sort of a fairy godfather."

"Did you get a hold of some crack or something stronger?"

"No, what are you doing now? Let's meet up somewhere."

"Sounds like you need a different drug dealer first."

"I swear I'm not on anything. It's friggin' unreal what this guy knows."

"Alright…alright, I'm just practicing. Let's meet at the Gran Saloon in Pearl River---sounds like we both might need a beer…you might need more than one."

"I think we both might need a shot to go with that beer."

***

While waiting for Don, I saw Benjamin walking through the doorway at the Saloon.

"Well, I'm glad you're here. Maybe you can help me convince Don of who you really are."

"Shit, just as I thought. I should have warned you not to tell him. This has to stay our secret if you hope to find Larry."

"Why is that? Is this just a test?"

"No, it's just that once people find out that one person has someone watching over them, everybody wants one. Then people would start misusing us for personal gain."

Benjamin, with his voice cracking and seemingly searching for his words, came closer to me. "Jim, I've got some shitty news, some bad news and what could be a little better news. I'm not going to ask you what order you want them in. It's hard enough to tell you."

"Okay, spit it out."

"The crack addict you thought, er, was Larry isn't him and he, um, died from an overdose last night. Ronnie is gone too, not dead, but just in limbo."

"You couldn't have told me about that addict two weeks ago? What is this, a fuckin' game for you?"

"I am not all knowing. I do have some powers but I'm not omnipotent. I can feel that Larry is still alive but I can't tell you where."

"So I wasted a couple of weeks thinking he was my brother. When you knew he wasn't, you son of a bitch."

"I could feel him close by…thought he would turn up if that wasn't him. Sorry, in case you didn't already know, life doesn't always go your way."

I'd seen enough disappointment especially when it came to the search for Larry. Hell, I think Larry's disappearance cut my mother's life short as did her problems with me. But, damn, this was so close.

"So, what happened to Ronnie?"

"You wouldn't believe me if I told you."

It was hard to believe that was coming from a guy who had recently told me he was my hundred-year-old great grandfather who was also my fairy godfather. I'd had a pretty open mind most of my life. It was just north of gullible.

***

Now, my friend Wayne Trimarchi, there was a skeptical guy. Wayne had become a little more open-minded that night we'd gone camping at Morphy Lake, a small reservoir just south of Mora, New Mexico. It's at about 8,000 feet and, as such, is subject to summer afternoon storms. We had barely gotten there and set the tent up when one hit. We got back in the truck, overlooking the lake, and saw a couple of firsts for either one of us.

Lightning hit a tree across the lake, splitting it open and setting it afire. I forgot who saw that first but both of us could see an object made visible only by the split Ponderosa pine. We could still see the smoke from where the rain had put the fire back out when we left the campsite to check it out.

What had been made visible by the lightning bolt was an oversized santos (New Mexican saint) carved into a tree. It was about ten feet tall, about eight feet longer than I had ever seen one before. Its spectacular detail was overshadowed only by the event's similarity to the burning bush incident in the Bible.

That was only the beginning of our day there. We had attempted, in vain, to hide some wood from the rain and spent a couple of hours attempting to light a fire, simultaneously chopping away the wet outside of the logs to get to the drier inside. It was soon dark and the stars began playing tricks.

It was like no psychedelic I'd ever done and both of us were cold sober. First, the stars in the Northern sky began coming closer and then backing further away like the beat of a heart. Both of us were watching that when I turned around and saw that the stars were forming geometric patterns in the Southern sky. They would alternate from circle to square to triangle, putting on a geometry class that Mr. Weskerna would have been proud of for about forty-two minutes, about as long as my high school math class.

With the fire finally lit, we got a fifteen-minute break before the UFO showed up. Its searchlights plied the tall pines at first, quickly and quietly making its way to the shimmering water. It was all over in two minutes when it took off after hovering over the lake momentarily.

***

"I think I would believe you, Benjamin. My friend Wayne would probably believe you, too."

Chapter 17

Costello, Not Presley:

Don came in the front door of the old Herb's Muddy Creek Bar as Benjamin departed out the back. The Gran Saloon, in its former incarnation, was a favorite New York State watering hole of our group when we were in high school. That and the Black Bull Pub were both in Pearl River.

***

After often beginning the evening at Binovi's in New Jersey, Mark "Pickle" Pascale, Lee Rubin, Ricky Siegel and I spent many nights in Pearl River. Ricky didn't even drink and he was as much fun to go with as anyone. Plus he could always drive home with not a second thought.

Pearl River is just over the border from Montvale, New Jersey and I had fun things to look back at in both saloons. I got maced in my eyes for the first time during a fight as a spectator in the Black Bull and met Veronica at Herb's just after I mooned someone at the table next to her's.

She stuck a cigarette, filter first luckily, in my buttcrack and dared me to try to smoke it. I was only able to keep it lit, actually singed a few hairs, when I exhaled.

***

"So, guess what, Don. Larry wasn't Larry and he OD'd last night. But wait 'til I tell you about Ronnie."

Don wasn't as disappointed as I was since he hadn't been as convinced as I'd been. "Sorry to hear that. So what happened to…?"

Crash!!! Smash!!! No, it wasn't an episode of Batman but someone hitting a parked car out front. Don went running to the window.

"Shit! Someone hit my car!"

Pearl River had more than just the two bars I'd frequented and this wasn't the first time an officer had heard an accident from his booth a couple of blocks away.

The driver came rolling out of his truck. "Who put that piece of shit in my way?"

"It wasn't a piece of shit before you hit it," Don said.

"Go back inside, both of you. I'll handle this," the cop said to Don and myself in a New York Irish brogue.

"This is the first time a cop ever advised me to go into a bar. 'You should buy us a drink'," I said knowing he'd probably be in the bar after his shift ended.

"Just get in there, you wiseacre. I'll take care of the insurance and everything."

"I can already envision the scene. Me getting pulled over later and telling the cop, 'But the other cop told me to go back into the bar."

Don smiled but was intent on the Irish cop getting his work done. He didn't take his eyes off the window until he saw the insurance change hands.

The car hadn't sustained a lot of damage since the drunk was only going about fifteen mph. Don took off home after getting in his car from the passenger side.

I was a little melancholy while driving home from the bar. I had been fooled again by someone who seemed to look like Larry. Maybe that was my punishment for not taking a more active role when Larry had disappeared. What should I have done? Moved back to New Jersey to join in the search? Back to the area where I never felt at home?

Leaving New Mexico where I felt like I should have been born from the moment I first got there? I'd never thought that was a good idea. I would have ended up killing myself or somebody else if I stayed in the New York area. Well, I did come back a few years later but not with the intent of staying long. It was a five-year plan and, while I met some good people in those five years, I was glad that I would be going back soon.

Then *Veronica* came on the seventies station and I thought of what Benjamin said had happened to Ronnie. In my own way, I felt kind of sorry for her as a she then her as a he, the tranny happily working on trannies who had now made one last metamorphosis. Now he was…I don't even know how to describe it.

Then I remembered that some stupid people thought the song's singer, Elvis Costello, was an Elvis impersonator since he'd become popular not long after The King had died. Or maybe that was just me, the only person stupid and out of touch enough to think that.

I could see parts of Ronnie in my fairy godfather but who knew if my intuition could be trusted. With the third Larry proving to be false and other past mistakes similar to the Costello-Presley debacle, I wasn't sure if turning my brain in for a newer model might not be a bad idea.

Chapter 18

Benjamin's Feeling:

"I have a good feeling about this trip, like I might actually find him," Larry Goodman said to Victoria Russell, the closest thing he'd had to a girlfriend in the past ten years. It was sort of a May-September romance with her being fourteen years his senior.

They were living in Manhattan, just a few blocks from Bellevue on the Lower East Side. It wasn't the greatest neighborhood but it also was not full of shooting galleries, crackhouses and burnt out cars like Bed-Stuy or The Bowery. A rent-controlled apartment allowed them to live there affordably with Larry only working sporadically and Victoria driving for Greyhound.

"I'd like nothing better for my last run," Victoria said. "Who knows, I might even retire in New Mexico."

"I appreciate your help, especially for the first few years when I couldn't work legally. Who would have dreamt that when we met in that Greyhound station that we would still be hangin' out with each other?"

Larry initiated a kiss which seemed to bring them closer from the inside than they ever had been.

"I thought that I was destined to lose my family, my friends, even my life 'til I met you. Still look like you're in your twenties."

"And Larry looks like you're in his thirties."

It was moving past first base when Larry suddenly put the force out at second. "We've got to get ready, any other time."

"Yeah, Larry's right. We've got our whole lives together."

Larry wasn't sure if he was doing this out of love or some sense of owing Victoria. "Yeah, Vicky. And Jim's been in New Mexico since '76, it can't be a bad place to be."

***

"You know, I might still be out west if not for Liz. I liked most things there," Don said to me on his patio in Spring Valley, New York. "Except for you."

"Nothing made me happier than when you left, not really, of course," I told Don. "I was not surprised, though, when you guys got divorced."

"Not as surprised as when I showed up with her as my wife instead of girlfriend."

"Yeah, that was a shocker but she was a good looking girl."

"You know, a little piece of me is still in New Mexico. It really was the Land of Enchantment in 1980."

"I get that, even though my body is here in New Jersey, my heart is totally in New Mexico."

"You could have left a leg there and still have had more of you in Jersey than most of us do."

"Well, if I lost weight then people might actually think that we're brothers and you know I'm not elated to be related."

Benjamin seemed to show up at the strangest times. "I've got some news."

"About Larry?" I asked.

"No, about missing aviator Amelia Earhart. Of course about Larry."

"I'm not sure if this is a game for you but it's not for us. What about Ron--?" Don asked.

"Your younger brother is leaving the area soon."

***

The Port Authority Bus Terminal on 41st St. and 8th Avenue in Manhattan was a busy place with throngs of commuters constantly

71

coming and going from New Jersey. Then there were the people on the westbound buses headed eventually for L.A. Larry and Vicky were on one of those busses but most of the present passengers would be exiting long before then.

"It's about 700 miles from Albuquerque to L.A," Larry said to Vicky." I'd like to check out the Pacific once I hook up with Jamie."

"My parents took us there when I was a kid but I was still coming down from seeing Mickey Mouse the day before. So I don't really remember much."

"Was that before Mickey divorced Minnie?"

"Huh?"

"Yeah, Mickey left Minnie in 1962. He thought she was fuckin' Goofy."

"Very funny. I could have Larry thrown off the bus for profane language."

"But you wouldn't do that to the love of your life." Larry reached for her.

"And don't touch me while I'm driving!"

"Alright, then, I'm gonna read for a while."

"Read about how to act in public," Vicky said, smiling in the mirror.

***

"Jim, you should go back to New Mexico in about a week, at least for a vacation," my fairy godfather said.

"Why, you think Larry's gonna be there?" I asked.

"Not Amelia Earhart or the Lindbergh baby?" Don added in his own special wiseass manner.

"Yeah, I get the idea that could be happening," Benjamin said.

"On a scale of one to ten, what are the chances?" I said, having grown a little bit skeptical.

"Almost eight. I would say about 7.92."

"Not even going to ask where you got that number. What about your tranny partner at...?" Don tried to press a little harder.

"Gotta go," said Benjamin. And my fairy godfather knew how to leave, probably better than he knew how to do almost anything else.

Chapter 19

Greyhound Rescue:

"So, you haven't been anywhere west of the Mississippi before? Even with all your driving?" Larry asked Vicky, navigating her way through the Lincoln Tunnel toward I-80 eventually.

"No and the furthest Larry has been was Miami for the '79 Super Bowl when I took you, huh?"

"Well, I hitched it to Chi-town once. Not sure if that's further than Miami. It sure seemed like it."

"Yeah, I had to drive there more than a few times. Didn't much care for the traffic."

"I got promised some money when I got there but it didn't pan out. So my memories of Chicago are cold, wet and hungry. Not something I'd like to repeat."

"Yeah, Larry can say a lot of things about me but at least you've been comfortable when you're with me."

"Maybe a little too comfortable sometimes." Larry reached for Vicky's leg and the bus driver lost her bearings for a second.

"Don't touch...!!!"

***

"Wanna go grab a bite?" I suggested to Don.

"I should stay home with Sue and Andrew. Haven't been home much."

"I can't argue with that. Guess I'll grab a bite and head home. Gettin' dark out."

I got into the van and wasn't sure if I would look for a place to eat on the side streets or head to 80 to get back in more familiar territory quicker. I got on I-80 towards the Garden State Parkway and was headed for some Fra Diavalo at Marconi's.

Just when my mouth was watering for some spicy marinara, I had a visitor. "Your brother doesn't think much of me, does he?"

Of course, it was Benjamin. Although it was the first time he'd shown up in my van, I was used to him just showing up.

"I'm getting' psyched for Marconi's and I'm eating alone. Don, he's just a little more skeptical than me, that's all."

"Anyways, I think Larry is on his way. Moving on to New Mexico."

"You sure? What is he looking for me? Not maybe Pittsburgh or Miami or somewhere in between?"

"He seems to be headed towards Pittsburgh. Oy, who would go to Miami to schvitz all summer."

"What's up with the Yiddish all of the sudden?"

"You forget that I've got a *Yiddishe kup*. It was my first language."

"I thought a *Yiddishe kup* was more of an attitude. It's okay as long as you use just a few words here and there. I wasn't raised in a *shtetl*."

"I'm feeling Larry very close; he's somewhere right near here."

"Where, where???" I asked the now vacant passenger seat.

Damn, that guy is flying. A muscle car passed me by doing at least eighty-five in the right lane, real dangerous in the crowded Jersey traffic.

"I hope he doesn't cut off that bus," I said to myself as the bus rolled over to avoid what I now recognized as a '68 Charger. My first car. I could tell by the round taillights on the escaping vehicle as opposed to the square ones on the '69.

Aah, that Charger. Got a few tickets in that and went to a few concerts. But the speeding tickets cost more than the concert tickets back then. I remember trading cars with Billy Post and his '68 Cougar

75

with a 351 back then and we were supposed to meet a couple of hours later. We didn't meet 'til many hours later when he beat me in a race with my own car.

Ahh…memories.

"That Greyhound's gonna' catch fire," I heard someone else yell as I pulled over to help out. About six or seven of us had stopped to help.

"This driver's gone. Jammed into the steering wheel. We'll leave her for last."

"This guy's gone too, looks like he was trying to reach and help the driver. But he got slammed into this pole."

His wallet had come loose but there was no I.D. in it anyway. I got a strange feeling around him.

Benjamin showed up again, encouraging me to look for the live people who could still be saved. The group of us got a few more out and a couple more made it on their own. Looked like just the driver and man in the front seat were the only casualties.

Benjamin was by the victim in the front seat. We made one more round to be sure there were no little kids hidden under the seats or anywhere then removed the two bodies.

The first responders had made their way through the unyielding traffic. In New Mexico, people got out of the way of cops and ambulances. Here, it was just a way to see better with the roads lit by their strobe lights.

Benjamin wouldn't leave as he said that Larry's presence was felt in the area. He had seen the driver's I.D. Badge.

"It was hanging on the lanyard but it was torn by the wheel so that the last name was unrecognizable. First name, definitely Victoria."

Luckily, no one else could see Benjamin now. He was examining the live victims in case he had missed a clue about Larry. He moved on to the dead passenger but quickly was done when he saw me getting ready to leave.

"Don't leave yet. Something strange is going on," Benjamin said.

"Oh, you think so? My fairy godfather seems to have taken on some of the characteristics of my first girlfriend who became a guy. And he's led me on several wild goose chases looking for my long lost brother over the past three weeks. I would say reality needs to set back in for a day or two."

"Even if it means that Larry could be found."

"Yeah, even that. I have to go to work in a couple of hours." I would talk to the cops to describe the vehicle then. Someone else would probably describe it as the General Lee from *The Dukes of Hazzard*. But they didn't know about the taillights. Or maybe someone did.

Chapter 20

Reality Sets In:

Functioning on only two hours of sleep, I wasn't much help at my father's office. We were working on the full-blown campaign of *Peanuts for Peanuts* and this part took a little more concentration for me.

"Dad, I need to grab a nap and come back this afternoon. I'm just worthless right now."

"What's going on with you, Jim? I know you'll come back and we'll still be able to finish this phase on deadline but you just seem like your mind is somewhere else."

"It's a girl, Dad. I met up with an old girlfriend and things seemed to spark again." Yeah, she tried to rob me twice and by the way she's now a guy. Oh, and also I met your grandfather who's now my guardian angel helping to look for Larry.

Sure, I could see me telling him the whole truth.

"Just remember to keep a balance in your life with work and play. You came back here from New Mexico to get a little more serious about work."

"Well, I think a relationship could be serious. I'm too tired to talk now. Can we continue this later?"

"Yeah, get some sleep. You okay to drive?"

"It's only five minutes away, Dad." Even it was five hours, I was still a much better driver than my father. He would always brag how he'd never been in an accident and I would inevitably ask if he'd ever looked in the mirror to see how many he'd caused.

***

The radio newscasters were talking about the bus crash on Route 80 the night before and how some heroes had helped rescue the passengers before the cops and rescue squads had arrived.

"...two casualties unidentified pending notifications of next of kin," said the voice on the radio as I turned the van off in front of my house.

Hey, if being a hero would get Benjamin off of my back for a couple of days, then so be it. I turned on coverage of the crash on the TV news and probably fell asleep within seconds of lying down.

After about four hours of sleep, I awoke with memories of bits and pieces of a dream I'd had. Of course Benjamin was in it. And I saw Larry, ten years older but definitely him, riding in the front seat of a bus.

That was all I could remember. Was Benjamin right about Larry being nearby last night? Did I even touch his dead body when we removed it from the bus?

"The driver was forty years old and they've figured out her last name. Russell," Benjamin said as he reappeared on my couch. "The rider they still have no idea about."

"What the hell, were you sneaking around the morgue last night? And still showing up in my dream. When do I get some time off from you?"

"I'm trying to be a *mensch* here and all I get from you is a lack of respect."

"I think you're more of a yenta. You're just trying to start trouble."

***

A westbound Greyhound was on its second leg of the journey to Los Angeles. The previous driver was sleeping on the bus instead of getting a hotel in western Pennsylvania like she usually did.

79

"That slowed us down picking up the other passengers from that wreck. Hopefully, another driver gets on the road to help everyone get back on time again," said the driver.

His front seat passenger was trying to fall asleep next to the previous driver. "Yeah, it would be tough to be on this bus more than two days."

"Where you headed to, New Mexico or maybe Arizona?"

"Yeah, but right now, dreamland."

***

"Dad, I never knew my grandfathers. Matter of fact, I only remember the one grandmother," I said upon my return to the office. "You remember your grandfathers, right? They probably didn't speak much English, huh?"

"Well, I only got to meet Grandpa Benjamin, my mother's father. While he was a talented carpenter, he had some idiosyncrasies and was into the occult."

"Bet the rest of the family didn't take that well, huh?"

"Not well at all; he became kind of an outcast although he was still respected for his age as far as I can remember. Why all the questions?"

"Did you ever hear him say anything about watching over future generations from the spirit world?"

"No, we weren't allowed to talk with him about things like that. And after my father died, we were struggling just to survive. Even before the Depression."

"Did he have any sexual proclivities?"

"Whaaattt?"

"I met sort of a guardian angel a few weeks ago. He said his name was Binyamin Benjamin Epstein and he knows a lot about our family. But I thought it was odd that he liked transsexuals. How…?"

Not much surprised my father. He had been around. Maybe a little more than he should have, but let's say he'd seen people with a lot of different lifestyles in his forty years of working with artistic types on Madison Avenue.

"Transsexuals. Not the ones who dress like the opposite sex but the ones who…?"

I could tell he was straining at the words. "Yeah, the ones who follow in Christine Jorgenson's path."

"My grandfather???"

"How did he die?"

"He was hit by a car. The transmission got him in the head. Think it was 1938"

"Maybe that caused a shift in sexual preference?"

Chapter 21

Dinner With the Family:

"Smells like salmon loaf," I said. My nose twitched and my stomach quivered with anticipation. I had to wrangle a dinner invite.

Sometimes it was good to work in the home office right next to the kitchen. Other times it could be more disturbing to my concentration and this was one of those times. I had two or three minutes to get a place at the dinner table before I had to get back to work.

Grandma Tessie, Susan's mother, was cutting tomatoes for the salad, and being a little hard of hearing, she wasn't aware of me preparing to work my magic as I entered the kitchen. I walked around in front of her to make sure that she could see me grab a lungful of the kitchen's aroma.

"Making some salad, huh?" I asked her. "What are you having with it?"

"You don't need to show me that impish smile," Tessie said. "You know exactly what I'm making."

"It wouldn't be salmon loaf, would it? It smelled sort of like it."

"Yes, it's salmon loaf. I think everyone is going to be here so I don't have that much."

"Oh, okay." I said and went to the office to institute my backup plan.

"Dad, can you call the house phone in a minute?"

"What are you doing? We have a lot of work to do."

"It'll just take a sec."

"Alright."

I went back into the kitchen to look over Tessie's shoulder. "What are you looking for, a sample?"

"Of course." The kitchen phone rang and I went over to answer it.

"Hello. Okay." I hung up the phone and told her that Meri and Margie wouldn't be home for dinner.

"Alright, we should have enough then. Want to stay?"

I told her that I wasn't sure but this time she could tell I was lying. "Around 5; 30, then."

I walked back around the corner into the office, "Thanks, Dad."

I got some more writing done before dinner and kept my fingers crossed that my sisters wouldn't show up pre-salmon loaf. A reasonable expectation but either way it meant that I would have to make sure that there was something else to eat.

Unless they really did have other plans. Not so unusual for two teenage sisters. If not I would have to make sure that they would have something to eat. Like pizza. Their favorite was right down the street.

***

The entrée was just coming out of the oven when I heard someone coming in the front door. I headed in that direction.

"Hey guys, salmon loaf for dinner. I'll buy you pizza if you go to Davinci's." I knew they didn't like my favorite dish that much anyway, so in my own weird mind set, I was doing both of us a favor.

"Sounds good, Jim," Margie said. They caught on right away. "We just came home to get something," she shouted towards the kitchen.

"Okay, see you later," Susan said.

"I don't know why you like that stuff so much, Jim," Meri said as the girls exited.

I made my way back to the kitchen. "So Jim has some exciting news. A new relationship is blooming," my father said.

"Oh, Jim, that's great! When do we get to meet her? You're such a nice guy. You deserve some happiness and a family of your own,"

83

Susan said. She didn't just say those things--it really mattered to her that I was happy.

"Let's not make more of this than what it is. Right now it was just one date which ended up lasting a weekend. The chances of me ever settling down with a New York Jewish girl when there are so many great girls in New Mexico are very…"

"A Jewish girl!" Susan had heard the magic word and nothing else after that. "You're going to marry a Jewish girl!"

Somehow the salmon loaf didn't taste quite as good as usual anymore. Instant karma had bitten me yet again. But at least nobody knew about Larry yet.

***

I made my way back into the office to get some more work done after dinner. I was just getting into a flow when Benjamin showed up.

"I can't get any work done if you keep bugging me," I said to him.

"But this is important. It's about Larry. But I need to know first if you are acquainted with any transsexuals."

"You can't find any on your own. And what did happen to Ronnie anyway?"

"I guess it's time that you knew. Ronnie is a part of me now. Not just spiritually but physically."

"Yeah, yeah. I know you had sex with her..er, him. My great grand…"

"No, it's more than just sex." He turned around and pulled down his pants to reveal the birthmark on his left cheek.

"But, but…"

"Yeah, it's on my butt. The same place where Veronica had that wine-colored birthmark."

"I don't get…"

"Not as often as I get some. But let me show you something else." He pulled his underwear up but the pants all the way down to show me his knee.

"But, but…"

"No, not the butt, the knee."

"You've got the same burn marks that she had from when the log rolled out of the fireplace. What are you getting tattooed to look like him?"

"Does that look like a damned tattoo?" he said as he pulled up his shirt. There was another boob growing in between the original equipment with my name "Jamie" tattooed on it. Benjamin left.

I tried to work a little more but my mind was on boobs and not peanuts.

Chapter 22

Ronnie's Metamorphosis:

The bus continued west, making its way across the flat plains of Western Illinois to an hour break in downtown St. Louis. Victoria was driving again.

"I know Larry's never been here before but there isn't really much to see," Victoria said.

"Yeah, I'm looking forward to stopping in St. Louis just to get off the bus for a while. How long 'til we get there?"

"It'll be about a half hour. The Mississippi is the last big river we'll cross. The rivers get smaller but the sky gets bigger in the West. I remember the first time I saw it."

"That was when you were a kid, before the operation?"

"Yeah, it was when my parents still thought that they could make me like Larry or any other boy. We climbed Gateway Arch, went to a baseball game at Busch Stadium and went fishing in the Big River like Tom Sawyer. All I could think about was being Becky Thatcher."

"It must have been rough for you having to pretend and not knowing if you would ever get to live the life you were really born into."

"Yeah, if only Larry would have been there to help me through!"

"Larry wouldn't have been born yet. I know I've asked you before but why do you put my name in your sentences when I'm sitting right here?"

"I don't know. It's just one of those things that make me different."

"Changing from a man to a woman after running away at age sixteen wasn't different enough?"

"I suppose that you're right. Hey, there's the arch, look." she pointed off to the right as we neared the bridge.

"That is pretty high. Too bad we can't check it out."

"Don't think I'd want to go there again but I know Larry would. Hey, look my name tag got switched with someone else's"

***

I had a difficult time sleeping, thinking about Benjamin's similarities to Veronica especially the one under his shirt. Veronica's boobs were the first set I'd seen more than once and the arreola seemed to be the same as when she was fourteen.

For some reason, my mind drifted to another time when I couldn't sleep. I'd been on a bus to New York from Albuquerque with some relatively crazy people and every time my eyes would shut, somebody would shout and wake me up.

We passed by Busch Stadium with the famous Stan Musial statue out front and I knew it was only a few minutes to the St. Louis station. I though of what I had done once before on a bus break while passing through eastern Oklahoma, downing a six pack of Bud in about ten minutes.

That had afforded me a little sleep on that trip so the strategy might work again. I was on the lookout for a liquor or package store but didn't spot one. So when the bus stopped, I asked a guy standing outside the bus station where the closest place was.

Calvin said he would guide me if I bought him a big can of Cisco malt liquor. I agreed and he took me through a couple of alleys to a store where I got a quart of MGD (my tolerance had gone down since the previous bus trip) and he got his Cisco.

We returned to one of the alleys with refreshments wrapped in brown paper bags and proceeded to imbibe. Quickly finishing, I hadn't even thought that someone could have been hiding there to mug me.

We walked back out and crossed the street, standing in front of the bus station when two cop cars rolled up and put Calvin against the wall.

"Get out of here!" one of the cops yelled at me. He could tell I was obviously a tourist. "Get back in the bus station. It's dangerous out here."

His partner slammed my drinking buddy against the wall then into the car.

"How much did he get you for?"

"Oh, just two bucks."

"You're lucky. The last guy got beat up and they stole his watch and wallet. Go get some gum to cover your breath and get back on your bus."

"Ok, thanks." I had already bought gum because I knew that the driver wasn't supposed to let you back on the bus if you smelled like alcohol.

What a strange time to think of that. Speaking of strange, here was Benjamin.

"Well, at least you weren't in my dreams last night. What brings you here this morning, Benjamin?"

"I came to tell you about Ronnie/Veronica and what happened. You deserve to know."

"That's fine. Jest don't lift your shirt up again. I appreciate you lettin' me in on the secret."

"So, as an Orthodox Jew, it was difficult for me to satisfy my, shall we say, different sexual tastes. I had to pretend to be someone that I wasn't for most of my life. Except when I was able to find a hermaphrodite for the evening without danger of being recognized." There were no sex change operations back then.

"Wow, I don't know whether to say what a cool great grandfather I have or how freakin' weird is that?"

"So, when I got hit by the trannie and died..."

"Tranny? Thought a car hit you!"

"Yeah, the transmission on the car. Quit interrupting. They offered me a deal..."

"Who is they?"

"I didn't get their names but just listen! They told me that I would get to watch over my family's future generations and get to love transsexuals like I want but they would get them back after a year."

"Get them back for what?"

"I gotta' go," and Benjamin disappeared.

***

Ronnie woke up in Folsom, not the prison but the small town in northern New Mexico. Just a little ways from Trinidad where he'd gotten the operation. He felt like something extremely weird had happened to him, aside from suddenly ending up 2,000 miles from home, but it seemed like all the equipment was in the right place.

Chapter 23

Looking for Jim:

"I was trying to find out if they'd identified the people killed in the bus crash the other night. I think that the rider may been my long lost brother," I said to the sergeant at the New Jersey state police barracks.

"They've identified the driver...," the sergeant was interrupted by me.

"Yeah, her last name was Russell. I helped to pull her out of the bus."

"Actually, that's what we thought at first but it turns out she was wearing the wrong lanyard. But we haven't identified the rider yet."

"Can you give me any kind of description?"

"Let me see some identification."

I handed him my driver's license, still from New Mexico. "Got your passport?"

"That's New Mexico, not Mexico. We're between Arizona and Texas north of Mexico." How many times had I explained that and the ability to drink the water there without getting sick! I had to show him on the map before he believed me.

"Okay, Mr. Goodman, alright. The decedent was about five feet eight inches tall with blue eyes and brown hair. Sound like he could be your brother?"

"No, he's got brown hair but he's about six-two with brown eyes."

I still needed to be sure that Larry was alive. While I believed in the afterlife, I didn't have any connections with anyone who contacted the spirit world at the moment.

***

"Wow, incredible!" I had never seen levitation done successfully nonetheless been a part of it. My friend Kim, we had lifted her above our heads just using two fingers from the hands of four people.

We had tried this more than a few times before unsuccessfully and I had begun to lose confidence in the fact that it would ever work. But Lee Rubin. Steve, Lynn and Kim's cousin had talked me into the fact that it could happen.

Admittedly, when it didn't work, oftentimes it was because someone lost focus either through tickling or losing the wording of the story. Steve, holding up Kim's head, told the story flawlessly this time of how the person had died and their soul was going to rise up.

None of the four of us broke the chain from the time Kim rose over four feet high with us kneeling around her. It took about five minutes to complete the task and we had cut back on the marijuana so as not to laugh in the middle of the levitation.

When she rose, it almost felt like she was going to leave our fingers and quickly float out the window. It was such an awe-inspiring moment that we all promised not to tell anyone else about it at school, except for people who we felt could be accepting of it.

"They're gonna think we were hoarding the shrooms or not sharing our purple haze," Lee said.

"When we barely did a couple of tokes," I added. There was only one person I told about it. Alice was goth before anyone even used the word and she got me to delve a little further into the spirit world with tarot cards and Ouija.

***

"Hello, is Alice Prentiss available?" I was trying to find her fifteen years later and my first call was to her parent's house.

"She's outside playing with her white rabbits," her mother said. "I'll go get her. Who is this?"

91

I told her who I was and Mrs. Prentiss seemed delighted that I was trying to find her. I had a way with my friends' parents even more than my friends sometimes.

"It will probably be good for her. She hasn't been back home too long."

That sounded strange but I didn't think too much of it. I just wanted to see if she still had her Ouija board since the used ones channeled the spirits better than brand new.

"Looking to see if your brother is still alive," Alice said, having graduated to reading minds. "Been a few years, huh?"

"Whoa, Alice, you never cease to amaze me. Wherever I was in the last fifteen years, I always felt like you were with me." I wasn't lying either. Sometimes I would turn around expecting her to be behind me and all I would get was a whiff of her unique perfume.

"Yeah, I was there from New Jersey to New Mexico and back to New York. You've had quite a life but I always knew it would lead back to me. And your great-grandfather."

"Y-y-you know Benjamin?"

"Sure , I live half in that world and half in this world. But sometimes the balance is thrown off. Hang on. It's time to sacrifice a bunny."

"S-s-sacrifice to who?" I was almost afraid to ask.

"Oh, I'm just messing with you. If I had gone to the dark side yet, I would have black bunnies," she let out her sinister laugh. "So you wanna try the Ouija board tomorrow night?"

"Love to. I'll come by around 11; 30 so we'll be ready for the witching hour. Sound good?"

"Of course. I made you say that."

I couldn't sleep that night since nobody that I knew or trusted could find out if Larry was alive, except Alice. We had a weird sort of connection. I trusted her to help me but neither one of us had visions of any more of a relationship than we already had.

Chapter 24

Making Contact:

I worked a few hours at my father's office in the morning but my mind was on my appointment with Alice. I had to work the dinner shift at the restaurant but asked my manager if I could get out early depending upon business that night.

It was busy early but sometimes that meant things would slow down after dark. Or sometimes it just stayed busy all night. Luckily that didn't happen and I was able to get my cleanup finished by ten o'clock.

That gave me about an hour and a half to prepare for and meet up with Alice. She lived far from the main roads in Woodcliff Lake and I knew it might be difficult to find in the dark. Jumped in the shower, then took off to her house a little early since I had to drive through the back side of Tice's apple orchards.

Most of the apples were gone off of the trees as far as I could tell in the dark. The only customers in the orchard were of the four-legged variety. A couple of raccoons and a few deer.

Speaking of which. I'd better slow down and stop looking for deer in the woods. I turned my head forward just in time to see a doe and her fawn crossing the road. Didn't have to skid to a stop but definitely had to slow down.

They came walking right up to the front of my van in the headlights. When the doe looked up, she had the face of a woman and

93

her fawn the face of a human child. I couldn't quite make them out because of the glare.

Turning the lights down to just parking lights, I suddenly recognized the face of the woman and her child. It was Mom and whoa...it looked like Larry. They began to sort of run ahead then come back like they wanted me to follow them. It seemed like they were leading me to Alice's house through the woods.

When I got there, they ran off. "You still like coming early even though you're fifteen years late," Alice said, or at least it sounded like her.

I couldn't see her but the glow of a fire was visible in the backyard.

"I was just gonna wait out here. I left early 'cause I wasn't sure of getting here at night," I yelled back.

"Of course you did. Come around back through the gate. I'm ready now."

"Where is …" Just as I was about to finish, the deer reappeared and ran up to point out the gate.

I opened the gate and could only see Alice's shadow. She looked ten feet tall. "Well, I guess my mother's spirit has already contacted me."

"Ah, you saw the deer I sent. Your mother running free with your brother."

"I should have figured you sent those. So does that mean my brother is dead?"

"Sit down, sit down and all will be told."

"What do we even need the Ouija board for. You already know the answers. Larry is dead, huh, Larry's gone." I let out a sigh mostly in sadness but at least a small part of which was relief that I finally could end my hunt.

"Just sit down so you can learn the whole story. The board will literally spell it out for you."

"I'm gonna go. Got what I came here for. Thanks for the help." Why couldn't she see that I needed some time to digest this. "I'll come visit again soon, I swear."

"Things might not be as they seem. Everything is a little grey in the afterlife, there's no black and white."

It didn't make sense. Was Alice just trying to keep me there? I could tell she didn't get a lot of visitors. "Alright, if you're telling me to keep an open mind, I will."

She got out the board, taking her time to treat it gently and turned the pointer over. She lit a few candles and we put our fingers on top of the planchette. "Great oracle, I am trying to contact Larry Goodman or Mazie Goodman. Are you there?"

The indicator moved down the board, away from the yes or no at the top. It drew us to five and then three.

We weren't sure, so I asked, "What does that mean, Ouija, 53 like 1953?" No movement for a few moments.

"Is this Mazie? Spell it out," Alice said. The pointer moved a little towards the letters, then stopped.

"Tell us! Tell us who this is," I said. "Mom, is that you?"

It moved again. This time landing on L, then A. I took my fingers off.

"It's Larry. It's him. I know it is."

"All is not as it might seem; put your fingers back on. Remain calm." I replaced my fingers on the planchette.

Alice apologized and asked if the spirit was still there. The pointer moved again to L, then A...N...D.

"L-A-N-D, what could that mean? The board misspells things sometimes but that still couldn't mean Larry. He was a good speller, too."

"That doesn't mean anything. It could be LALAND with 53 before it," Alice theorized.

"Mom, I know you're nearby. What does this mean. Who is there with you?"

The pointer moved again, this time to M, then A...Z...I...E. "Mom, I'm sorry. I know you were having a rough time but I should have apologized to you."

95

YES, the board said. It spelled out B-R-O-T-H-E-R. "Larry," I yelled.

NO, the board said. L-E-L-A-N-D D-I-E-D. "Who? I don't know Leland," I asked. "We didn't have a brother named Leland."

S-E-C-R-E-T D-I-E-D 1953. "We had a brother who died before I was born?"

YES. I had always thought it was strange that my parents had waited that long to have me.

It took a while but we found out that Leland was named after a WW II buddy of my father's who'd died on D-Day. But there was no info on Larry. Every time we asked, the oracle would shut down and not move until we changed the subject.

"Is my mother stopping him from talking or is he still alive? What do you think, Alice?"

"I'm not sure."

Chapter 25

Change of Plans:

"Don, I think Larry is on a bus to New Mexico as we speak," I told my brother. "I'm probably going there next wa..."

"Next week! We were going to try and take the first load of stuff to Vermont next week. You promised me. What, is that crazy fairy godfather telling you stories again?"

"Well, he hasn't really stopped but I felt something myself. It was when we were helping people after that bus crash and I thought that Larry might have died in it."

I explained how my mind had changed to think that Larry would be in Albuquerque.

"And Benjamin helped you to feel that way, of course."

"Well, at first he made me feel like it was Larry who died but then I went to the state police and the description of the unidentified body didn't fit."

"So he might be dead, might be alive. Might be in New York, might be in New Mexico. Doesn't sound like Benjamin has his shit together."

"He's got it more together than Ronnie does. I don't know how to describe it but Ronnie is mainly a part of Benjamin now. Apparently our fairy godfather made some sort of a deal with the devil."

"I think you are, too, if you listen to that guy."

"He's been watching over our family since Dad first went off to war. I figured he deserved some benefit of a doubt."

"I doubt that."

***

Benjamin looked at his body and saw the remnants of the other transsexuals he'd had affairs with in the past. It wasn't a bad trade-off he'd made just to be scarred with their markings. He was sort of a step above *The Illustrated Man* whose afterlife was told in not just pictures but actual pieces affixed to his body.

There was Georgy's penis affixed right next to his own. She had been the first and only one he had known in real life. Georgy had died right after Benjamin had when a straight man had been shocked by her equipment. Being a mortal, she was long gone now but she'd got to have a happy life.

But there were memories of the other eleven he'd been with in the fifty-plus years since he'd taken on his guardian angel position. Ah, he thought, I got the best parts of all. If I ever get bored I can just play with myself.

And, after all, they got to live in the body they'd always really wanted to without having to take those hormones.

***

"Morning, any chance that I could work for a meal here?" Ronnie said to what appeared to be the owner of the Folsom Café.

"Not too much going on today. Where you from, *amigo*?" Duke said.

Being from New York and relatively pale-skinned, Ronnie was taken aback by being called *amigo*. "Um, originally from back east but I'm traveling through looking for a new place to settle. I figured there had to be something good about this place since this was where the first cavemen settled in North America." He was really planning on going to Albuquerque, at least. If not back to New York.

"Oh, you read the sign across the street, did you? Well, it pays to do your homework. Unfortunately there's not much going on here."

Just then, a tour bus pulled up at Joe's Garage next door. It didn't sound or smell like it was running right

"I know that smell. That's the smell of money. Kind of like what the rancher said to the city feller who asked how he put up with the smell of cattle shit. No, the rancher said, that's the smell of money; it's easy to put up with. I might be able to use you today, after all."

***

"It sure is different driving through the West," Larry said as the bus left Amarillo headed for New Mexico. "I thought that it was a long ways between Tulsa and Oklahoma City but now there's nothing but wide open spaces for as far as I can see."

"Yeah, that and the giant cross we passed a few miles back," Victoria said. "I'm praying you find your…"

'Hey, look, what the hell…?" Larry pointed to an odd formation of cars buried nose first on the south side of I-40.

"Oh, that's the Cadillac Graveyard. Some rich rancher got new Caddies every year and buried the old ones," a passenger behind Larry said. "Worth stoppin' at when you got the time."

"Crazy shit," Larry said. "We shouldn't be too far from Albuquerque. Where's Jamie's address?" He rifled through some papers and fell asleep.

Chapter 26

Jamie's Destiny:

"Benjamin, you sure that Larry's gonna' be in New Mexico if I go there? I'm changing my whole schedule around to do this," I told my (not always great) great-grandfather.

"I'm so sure that I'll close up the damned shop for the weekend and come out there too," he responded.

"Really, how would you get there? Matter of fact, how do you get around? Do fairy godfathers fly like angels? When I lose a tooth, will you leave…?"

"I'm not the damn Tooth Fairy but I'll knock your fuckin' tooth out if you ask me too many more questions. Don't worry about how I'll get there. I will get there!"

"Who does the work when you're not at the shop anyways? Seems like you're never there."

"Don't you worry, I'll get things done."

I told Benjamin emphatically that all the magic he'd worked so far had made my job and personal life almost disappear.

"We're hot on the trail and I got your transmission fixed, didn't I?"

"Maybe you should be fixed so you can concentrate on Larry instead of your next transsexual conquest."

"I know you've learned that anything worthwhile takes a little sacrifice. But, and I emphasize the but, you must have some fun along the way. I've watched you do that all your life, too."

"That's the trouble; you're always emphasizing the butt especially if it's on a trannie."

***

The tour bus was full of Texans headed back to Dallas after checking out northern New Mexico's ancient history. They had just left Capulin Volcano and were due for a short stop to see the remnants of Folsom Man when the bus messed up on them. Their last stop was to be Clayton Lake State Park's dinosaur tracks before they headed southeast to Texas.

"Just avoid talking to those Texans if you can. They'll give you a hard time about your New York accent," Duke said to Ronnie.

"You can wait on them anyway; I'll help in the back until it's time to cle...," Ronnie said.

"You learned how to cook chicken fried steak and biscuits with gravy or huevos rancheros in New York City?"

"I'm not from the city but no, I never even ate any of that."

"Then you're waitin' tables."

"I'll put on my best Southern drawl if it means I get to eat. Can I get something quick now before they come?"

"Yeah, I'll fix you up some *papitas a la* Duke. That would be the Spanish a la because that's what people say when they taste 'em. A la, those potatoes are good."

"Alright, I'll try anything."

"I'll make 'em mild since you probably haven't ever ett spicy food."

"Whatever, I'm just hungry."

"Oookay." He added the onions and peppers to the potatoes already on the grill.

But Ronnie hadn't noticed the green chile mixed in with the bell peppers. His eyes were tearing when he commented on how strong the onions were.

"The onions might be strong but the chile's a little stronger," Duke said.

The tourists were on their way over. "I'd better eat now before they fill this place up," Ronnie said while Duke was throwing some more potatoes and meat on the grill to prepare for the rush.

"Here you go."

"Thanks," Ronnie said as he took a big shovelful in his mouth. That was the last thing he could say for the next five minutes as he ran for some water.

"A little hot?" Duke said with a smile. He went to get some milk and poured a little chocolate syrup in it. "Here, that'll help more than water."

"Aahh...that's a lit...," Ronnie tried to say as he poured the soothing solution onto his tongue.

The door opened and in came the tourists. The café filled up quickly... about thirty seconds for thirty customers.

At least Ronnie wouldn't have to worry about the Texans catching his accent. The chile had his mouth paralyzed. He could hear Duke laughing in the kitchen.

Chapter 27

Looking for Jamie:

I can definitely see why Jamie stayed here," Larry said while staring at the mountains all around him. The bus made its way through Tijeras Canyon.

"Yeah, while Larry was hiding in plain sight his brother was out in the middle of nowhere," Victoria said. "Did you ever think that we'd be here? A few months ago…"

"Fuck the past. We're here now."

"Larry a little nervous? I know that I am, mostly for you."

"It'll all work out. Sorry for jumping on you. I know that I made some mistakes in the past. I just hope that Jamie can get past all that."

"No doubt he's made some mistakes too."

"Well, maybe I should have come to New Mexico ten years ago. I could have lived here but then we probably wouldn't have met."

Vicki grasped his hand a little tighter.

"2801 Monroe NE is where we're headed to next. That's Jamie's address I got from my mom just before she died."

***

"Wouldn't that have been something if Larry would have been in New Mexico in 1980? The Goodman brothers would have all been together... maybe you would have stayed there, too," Jim said to Don on the front step of his brother's ranch style home.

"Yeah, then maybe you wouldn't be going on these wild goose chases all around the country. I wouldn't have met Sue or had Andrew if I had stayed out there. Life is good for me now," Don said.

"Maybe the two of you could have teamed up and beaten me in basketball. I know you could never do it alone." I picked up the ball sitting in Don's driveway and took a shot at the basket above his garage.

"You were definitely better than me when you were younger. Now…"

"Yeah, I know. I'm just too wide for you to get around. Right…I'll still kick your ass in Horse or 5-3-1. Whatever game you wanna' play."

"No time to kick a horse's ass' ass in horse especially since you're not helping me take a load to Vermont."

"I got you some help, what are you crying about now? You just need an excuse."

Don might have had an excuse not to play basketball but I'd always had an excuse to play basketball. It was my outlet. The one place that I could go where other kids wouldn't give me a hard time about my buck teeth.

***

Bucky Beaver, Human Can Opener. There were lots of different names. While I could still hear them a lot of the time, even when I was alone, I could never hear them when I was shooting hoops.

And I got pretty good at it by the time I was in seventh grade. The high school kids would let me play full court with them a lot of the times. But only if I could answer a trivia question, usually about baseball since it was mostly during the summer when we played.

"Who's the third-string shortstop for the Montreal Expos?" they would ask me.

"Well, everybody knows that Bobby Wine is the starter and baseball's top base stealer Maury Wills is behind h…"

"Come on, who's third string?"

"That's gotta' be Garry Jestadt." And out on the court I'd go with the bigger guys. If I'd make a shot or a good pass, they'd give whoever was covering me a hard time. But that was back when I was still Jamie.

***

"Does Jamie Goodman live here? Are your parents home?" Larry said to the little girl through the locked screen door.

"Jamie who…uh…no. And nobody home 'cept my brother Boomer. He asweep," said seven-year-old Cindy Dautel. She was a cute little girl who had yet to learn how smart she really was.

"Here's my phone number at the Zia Motor Lodge. Can you save this for your parents?" Larry slipped a piece of note paper from their current abode with a dollar bill through the crack in the door.

"Thank you," Victoria said as Cindy put the scrap in her pocket.

"Wow! A whole dollaw." She knew that money meant candy.

"What's your name?" Victoria asked.

"I'm Cindy, I'll tell my pawents you wa hewe."

"You won't lose that number either, right, Cindy?" Victoria said.

"No, I have it wight hewe." Cindy reached her hand into her pocket and pulled it out.

"Bye-bye," Victoria said and Cindy waved with the number still in her hand. She closed the door and her thirteen-year-old brother Boomer came out of his room still half asleep.

"Did I hear you talking to somebody?" Boomer said to Cindy.

"Yeah, some people were looking for a guy named Jerwy Gorman and they wrote their numbew down for Mom and Dad. Hewe," Cindy said and handed him the paper.

That really did no good because Boomer was dyslexic and, although he had a 180 IQ, he still could not read a lick. "Just give it to Mom when she comes home. You didn't unlock the outside door, right?"

"No, I just talked to them through the scween doow." She got the note back from her brother and put it on the phone table near the front door; nowhere near as safe as the dollar she put in her pocket.

***

105

"It would have been cool if Jamie would have been there. But nothing is easy, Vicki," Larry said.

"No and everything is even a little tougher for Larry."

"I guess we just go back to the motel and wait for a call."

"Yeah, I'm feeling pretty good that they'll get the message and Jamie will call."

Chapter 28

A Comedy of Errors:

"Well, son, you made it through the whole meal without dropping a plate or spilling a water. Here's ten bucks. You want some more of those *papitas*?" Duke said to Ronnie with a grin from ear to ear.

"Thanks but no thanks on the *papitas* but I wouldn't mind trying some chicken fried steak. Not spicy please!"

"Don't worry; it just comes with cream gravy on top. Unless you want a little green chile mixed in. It's really good that way." Duke breaded the cube steak and put it in the pan to fry.

"No, that's alright. Just some mashed potatoes with that gravy. That will cool off my stomach."

The café owner flipped the cube steak and put the potatoes and a fresh roll onto the plate along with some green beans. He placed it under the heat lamp until the steak was ready.

"So when did you get the operation?" Duke asked Ronnie.

"Huh…what op…?"

"The sex change, what other operation would I be talking about? You think that you're the first transsexual I've seen? We're only about fifty miles from Trinidad."

Ronnie was pretty amazed that Duke knew anything about sexual reassignment living in the middle of nowhere like he did. "How could you tell? Dr. Biber worked on me in 1982 but I just recently was able to stop taking my hormones."

"Just call it transgadar. After the doc helped me out in '65, I just developed that power." He put the overflowing plate down on the counter in front of Ronnie.

"What…really…you!!"

"Yeah, it was tough back then and I came from a small town but not as small as Folsom. Eunice is in the southeast part of the state. Not many people knew what was wrong with me when I left and it was tough deciding to never go back, But Deuce Aspades died a long time ago."

"Wow, that's a strange name. Like a riverboat gambler."

"Well, my daddy ran an illegal poker game where he would get the oilfield workers' losings."

"You've had an interesting life, huh?"

"You don't know the half of it, son. I met ma first wife in Trinidad and she used to be a man. Everybody 'round here has kids 'cept for us. This strange guy Benjamin got us together back…"

"Bennnnn...jamin," Ronnie said, shuttering at the thought. "I met up with an old man named Benjamin recently and had some dealings with him. Guess this area would be the best place for a guy with his strange sexual tastes."

A local walked in to the restaurant, greeting Duke who motioned Ronnie to change the conversation.

"Cup a joe, John?" Duke asked.

"No, gotta use your john before the joe, Duke. Gonna have to get down to Albuquerque for those tranny parts. Damn 4-wheel ain't kickin' in!"

"Transmission problems? I work on transmissions. What kind of truck you got?" Ronnie said.

"Who's the kid?" John asked Duke.

"He's just passin' through but he helped me get through a busy lunch. Seems nice enough. Can't hurt to have him look at your Suburban."

108

Ronnie asked, "What year Suburban is that?"

"It's an '85. Less than 100K…"

"The transfer case was a problem that year. I'll look at it for free and it should be a cheap fix. Maybe for a ride to Albuquerque."

"Son, I'd give you a ride to New York if you got my tranny fixed today. *Vámonos.*"

Luckily, John had made a move for the door so Ronnie figured out what he was saying.

"A tranny who works on trannies. What will they think of next?" Duke said to himself as the pair left. "Good luck," he added out loud.

***

I got in John's car to head to the airport. John Krall was a reliable friend who made me happy I had moved to New York State to help my father out. He was ten years younger than me but had learned some of life's lessons before I had.

"You really think your brother might be in New Mexico, Jimbo?"

"I don't know, Johnny, but it's worth checking out if there's even a small chance."

"This guy Benjamin doesn't seem that trustworthy. I think that I would have to side with your brother being skeptical of him."

"I don't know. I just get a feeling that he's right. If I didn't check, there would always be this feeling in my craw that I had not given finding Larry a chance."

The storm front moved in as we approached Newark International Airport. Right on cue, the news came across the car's radio that flights would be delayed.

"Want to go back home, Big Jim?"

"Nah, I'll just wait at the airport. It should clear up soon enough."

Chapter 29

A Comedy of Errors – Part Two:

A gentle breeze wafted through the Bel-Air neighborhood where the Dautel house at 2801 Monroe NE was located. It was a peaceful day with cottonwood blossoms riding that breeze. Until the pressure tightened down in the afternoon. And the forty mph winds brought the sands like little missiles to knock down the blossom hitchhikers.

The note Larry Goodman had left for his brother floated off of the phone table onto the floor and was found by Annie Dautel where it was carefully archived in the round file.

"I helped you clean up, mommy," said the nine-year-old Annie to her mother, Linda Dautel.

"Here's a quarter for helping," Linda said. "Can you take the bag out?"

"Okay, mommy." And the crumpled paper on top blew down the street as quickly as anything else caught up in the monsoonal winds.

Cindy reentered the room and immediately went to the table looking for the piece of paper. "Mommy, did you see a piece of papew hewe?"

"No, but I was cleaning."

"Do you know somebody named Jerwy Gormson? They weft a message fow him."

If I hadn't left three years previous, Linda might have recognized the similarity to Jimmy Goodman. What the Dautels called me. "No. Couldn't have been anything too important. He'll come back if it means that much."

***

I was a little nervous as the Continental jet approached Denver for the second leg to Albuquerque. Not nervous about the flying, I'd done that a few times but nervous about finding Larry. What would I say to him, What if I said the wrong thing. One of my specialties?

I'd had two Budweisers on board and needed to make room for more. But I hated airline bathrooms. As we neared the Mile High City, I thought about how cramped it would be to join the Mile High Club on this plane. Of course, the plane always hit enough turbulence while I was in the bathroom to spoil my aim. And there was barely enough toilet paper to wipe the seat off so the next person, if it were a woman, wouldn't get my splashback.

Just when it was time for me to leave, there was a tap on my shoulder. "Dammit, Benjamin! Can't you leave me alone? Guess you got used to looking for love in all the wrong places."

"Just checking up to see how you're doing. I hope you're not mad but I don't think Larry is in New Mexico anymore."

"You old sonuvabitch. Are you just playing games with me? I can't fuckin' believe you dragged me across the country for no good reason."

"Now, that's no way to talk to your great grandfather/fairy godfather. Besides, I'm just kidding. Stronger feelings are coming through."

"Funny, very fuckin' funny."

"You should check at your friend Jack's house when you get to Albuquerque. I saw his family in a vision."

"Yeah, I see a vision of you with your head smashed in by that transmission in 1938." I went to exit the bathroom but the door wouldn't unlock.

"You wouldn't have gotten this far without me, would you?"

"Yeah, I got far. My brother Don is pissed off and he's just at the head of a long line of family members and others who are a bit skeptical about..."

"Don't worry, he's there. See you in a couple of hours in Nuvo Mexico."

"Yeah, why don't you go now and work on your Spanish. It's *Nuevo* with an e and *Mexico* where the x sounds like an h."

"Hasta le pasta. When you work on your Yiddush, I'll work on my Spanish."

"*Shalom*, mother fucker let me out the fuckin' door."

"That's Hebrew!"

Chapter 30

Smooth Landing:

I changed Continental planes in Denver, as usual, and got a window seat since it was light out and you could usually follow the Rockies for the whole hour-long flight. The first of the snowcapped peaks had me realizing that I could even see Larry in the airport when I landed in just an hour.

So I knew the window for obtaining alcohol was a small one. I rang the button and asked, "Can I get two beers before last call?"

"You'll need to drink them fast," said the stewardess. "But there's no reason to be nervous. We have a very competent pilot and staff."

"Oh, no. Not afraid of flying. I could be meeting up with my brother who's been lost for ten years."

"Wow, guess I might be nervous too."

"Yeah, I actually haven't seen him in thirteen years. He was only thirteen years old then and I'm sure he's changed a lot."

"Good thing you're not triskadecaphobic. Maybe thirteen will be your lucky number. I love a good mystery and will be in Albuquerque a few days. Want some help?"

"Maybe, but I'm not sure when." What are you kidding me? It's like every man's dream to hang out with a hot stewardess who'd be leaving in a few days.

"She handed me a piece of paper and winked. "Just let me know."

She was probably a member of the Mile High Club. I just hoped that small bathrooms weren't all she was used to. Could have used a third beer then but while a part of me was ascending the plane was already descending.

***

Ronnie got the wire hooked up to the transfer case correctly and John's Suburban was back on the road.

"Can you wait 'til tomorrow for that ride? Got some things to take care of that I couldn't do without a car."

"Sure, can you just bring me back to Duke's? I'm sure I can hang out there and maybe earn another meal."

"No problem; pick you up *mañana*."

"See you tomorrow," Ronnie guessed at what he meant. "Oh, wait. You're still taking me over there."

"Yeah," John said with a smile. "I'll be ready in a minute if your New Yawk ass can wait that long."

"I'm waiting. So you ready yet? How about now?"

"Very funny. Hang on to your britches."

"I'll go wait in the truck."

"Okey-dokey. It'll probably be faster that way anyways."

By the time John had gathered up a list of errands and combed his hair, Ronnie was already asleep in the front seat. He looked so comfortable that the cattleman just drove in to town from the ranch and left him in the Suburban while doing his errands.

"Duke, that boy tuckered himself out but got my transmission fixed. I'm leaving him to sleep in the truck whilst I do some errands. You'll be here for a while?"

"Oh yeah, don't imagine he got much sleep last night."

"I'll buy him a meal when he wakes up; he's earned it." John went to the feed store, then parked the car in the shade of Folsom Prison, a local watering hole sporting a Johnny Cash theme. In the town of Folsom and near everywhere else in New Mexico, you got your shade where you could. Unless you were in the forest there weren't very many trees to grab shade from. What small amount of trees planted in parking lots usually had their shade taken by employees of whatever stores or offices in said plaza. And the same went for the scarce amount of tall buildings.

***

Ronnie woke up a little disoriented since he had never been in the alley next to that bar. He quickly figured out, upon exiting the Suburban, that John's errands mainly involved meeting a few different people at the bar after picking up a couple of bags of feed. With *Ring of Fire* playing at just the right level from the jukebox, Ronnie could hear his driver's voice from inside the establishment.

"That New Yawker did a heck of a job on my tranny, had it fixed lickety split. Joe, you should try to hire him at the garage so folks wouldn't have to go to the city to get their trannies fixed."

"Jest don't know how much call I would have for transmission work on a regular basis. Can he do any other kind of wrenchin'?"

"I don't know that he can, but he sure was handy with that transfer case." John lifted the draught to his mouth and took the foam off the top of his beer.

Joe sipped on his Jack and Coke and swirled the glass' contents while gazing into it for an answer. "Lessee what else he can do and didn't you say he wanted to go to the big city."

"That's right," Ronnie said as he strode in. "Can you spot me for a glass of Chardonnay, John?"

"Chardonnay!!! That's some kind of white wine, ain't...?" the bartender spit out his drink of questionable ancestry. It looked like it could just be a Sprite but smelled more like a gin and tonic as it shot out of his mouth across the bar. "We don't got no fancy wine here. Jest a cheap red table wine. Ain't worth wastin' fridge space on wine."

"Can you mix some of that red with some 7UP on i...?"

"This guy cain't be no good as a mechanic. I have never seen where those two W's, wine and wrenching go together," Joe said and the bartender laughed. Just then, the water shot up from the glass cleaning sink right into Rick the bartender's face causing everyone to laugh except for Ronnie, and Rick of course.

115

Ronnie came around the bar and first got the water turned off. Then he looked at where the leak had come from, found some extra hose and clamps then patched it up. "You'll need to get a more permanent fix later but this should work for now."

"Here's your red wine and 7, on me. I guess you can fix things up besides transmissions," Rick said.

"Yeah, but I still want to head to Albuquerque." Ronnie had a satisfying sip of his drink knowing that he had won over the denizens of Folsom Prison. Sometimes it's better to leave a place with a good reputation than stay around long enough to ruin it.

Chapter 31

Larry Goes to the Mountains:

"I wish that I knew where Jamie might hang out so that I could go there and look for him. I hate just sitting here and waiting," Larry said in their room at the Zia, an old Route 66 motel which still had its neon in working order.

"Maybe Larry and I should go see the town a little bit. I don't know if we should go back to that house again and bother them yet," Victoria answered.

"I'm sure Jamie will call once he gets the message. Unless he just didn't give a shit about me. My mom used to say he didn't but I think he just didn't come around because of her."

"From what you've told me about your mother, I know that she had her days. I just can't imagine your brother not caring about Larry."

"Well, I remember that he came around with some food in the afternoon sometimes before we left Hillsdale. He would always try to come before Mom got home from work, though."

"You didn't see him much after you moved to the apartments, huh?"

"Just the one time when he picked me up right before he moved out west...er...here. It was 1976 and I was thirteen."

"And your other brother?"

"I saw Don quite a bit until I left. But he was in some trouble...when I last saw Mom, she said he had moved west too. But his address was tougher to find. She thought he had moved back to New Jersey but wasn't sure."

"She was a little confused right before she died, eh?"

"Yeah, let's move on to a happier subject. We should get out of here for a few hours."

"We can just tell the desk clerk to take a message if there are any calls. Give him a couple of bucks and I'm sure we could get a transvestite hooker if we wanted."

"Not today, let's go check out the mountains. We could hike or take the tram they have all these signs about."

"Let's see how expensive the tram is and then we can hike around at the top of the mountains."

"I got a feeling it's not going to be cheap but let's check it out."

"We can just cruise up there in the rental car and if it's too expensive, we can take off hiking just a little north," Victoria said while looking at the map she'd picked up from the front desk.

"You've got the money so if that's what you want to do."

"It's our money, not mine. I don't want you to feel like you owe me for whatever I put out."

Larry reached over and grabbed Vicky's leg. "We could just stay here and see if you'll put out," he said, grinning.

"It's a beautiful day out. We can always come back here later or fool around on top of the mountains."

"As long as you'll let me get on top while we're on top. Let's go. You talked to the clerk already, right?"

"Of course." The phone rang right on cue so obviously the clerk hadn't gotten it.

Larry answered saying "Romero, wrong room."

The pair stopped by the front desk to straighten out the phone issue and found the clerk trying to hide a bottle of Wild Turkey he'd been sipping on. "Okay, we're leaving now so be sure to get the phone," Larry said.

"Here's another five bucks," Victoria said. "Don't forget. It's real important."

The ride towards the mountains on Central and then along the foothills on Tramway Blvd. was breathtaking for the pair as they had never seen anything that tall back East. The Sandias, near the southern terminus of the Rockies, dwarfed the forests of skyscrapers in Manhattan. When the pair got to the Sandia Peak Tramway, the price was only fifteen dollars. Cheap by New York standards.

There was a short line waiting for the next tram to come. But the fresh air and scenery unique to Larry and Victoria was enough to keep their wheels spinning. They would look forward and then to both sides.

"Look at the view of the city behind us," Victoria said. "I'll bet that would be something at night."

"Yeah, that would be cool." Larry said as the tram car pulled up and began to unload.

"A little breezy up there. Get ready for an interesting ride," said an anonymous passenger as he disembarked.

"Yeah, I wouldn't wait too long to come back down since those winds will really kick up this afternoon," said another. "It can get like a carnival ride up there."

"That would really make it worth the fifteen bucks," Larry said.

"And away we go," Victoria said.

It was only a few minutes up to the top of Sandia Peak but Larry was quickly reminded of his last time in a moving vehicle up that high.

"This feels like the morning before the Super Bowl all over again. Watching from the Goodyear Blimp as the Steelers got ready to kick some Cowboy butt."

"Whaaaat? You got to go up in the Goodyear Blimp. I knew you went to the game but how did you ever get a ride in that thing?"

"I was just in the right place at the right time. Had my trusty yellow towel and was the only Steeler fan in a group of Cowboy fans when they asked if someone could show the best symbol of loyalty to each team."

119

"And your Steeler towel was the best thing anyone could come up with?"

"Yeah, it had a little blood on it from when a Cowboy fan punched me the night before outside a bar. I told them it was Dallas quarterback Roger Staubach's blood...almost got punched again but it got me a ride on the blimp."

"Wish I had a picture of that."

"I had one but it got lost over the years. Anyways that was then and this is now. We're probably higher up in this car than I was in the blimp over Miami."

Chapter 32

They Meet:

Wayne Trimarchi and a couple of other old friends picked me up at the airport and had a cooler full of ice cold Buds, MGDs and George Killians (my favorite) in the trunk.

"When we gonna' drop your fat ass off so we can make room for the beer up here," were the first words out of Wayne's mouth. I'd like to say he was half-kidding but I think he was about ¾ serious. It was always hard to tell with him.

"Where'd you get this piece of shit, anyway?" I asked about his dirty, white late '80s Hyundai. "I could probably walk home faster. Just give me two beers."

"I'd say that was a three-beer walk. Where you goin' anyways?" said our other friend Jeff.

"Not sure. Guess I'm just stayin' with whomever's lucky enough to have me," I responded.

"You mean whoever wants to hear you burp all day and fart all night," Wayne said.

"You don't exactly smell like peaches and cream. Pull over so I can get another beer. I need to catch up to you guys," I said.

We drove around for a few hours discussing old times and checking out the old stompin' grounds and hangouts. Albuquerque had changed, even since my last visit. Only a year earlier.

Empty lots were filling in, my favorite bars were closing down or changing names and the streets were just busier. Tramway Boulevard was a perfect example of how much things had changed in the past year with new subdivisions blocking the views of the mountains springing up everywhere.

"Man, how this road has changed since I first came. It was dirt from Route 66 all the way up to Montgomery where it changed to pavement...," I said.

"Blah, blah, blah...yeah and then they paved it and you sold shit to the guys building the wooden pedestrian bridges over the top. Heard it all before," Wayne said.

He was deaf in his left ear. "Guess I was on your right side when I told you that."

"Where you headed now? Guess there's only one place this far up on Tramway, Juan Tabo Picnic Ground?" I said.

Wayne responded. "Yuppers, of course. Hey, look at those fools crammed into that tram coming down. They think they're seeing Albuquerque."

"We'd best check the beer situation before we go any further. Ain't no stores up there," Jeff suggested.

"You do think every once in a while, don't you," Wayne said.

"Only about selected subjects," Jeff said with a smile on his face.

I added, "Last time I looked, we were running low. Let's just turn around and go back to that last store on Montgomery."

***

The combination of altitude and dryer air was getting to Larry and Victoria as they stepped off the tram. Even though they'd had a drink at the High Finance Restaurant on top of Sandia Peak while they were watching the hang-gliders swoop down on the thermals, they were presently parched.

Vicky said, "Boy, a cold beer would really hit the spot now."

There were drinks inside the souvenir shop at the tram but nothing that would satisfy either one of them.

"Where's the closest place to get a six-pack?" Larry asked the clerk after buying a few souvenirs.

"Turn left when you come out of here onto Tramway and go about three or four miles south. It's on the left side. Grab me a quart while you're there."

"What time do you get off work?" Larry asked, thinking that it might not be bad to know someone local who could show them around.

"Serious? I'll meet you in the parking lot in a half hour."

Larry and Vicky walked outside where Vicky asked Larry if he thought the clerk was old enough to drink.

"That didn't stop you when I was underage."

***

I was in the store waiting to use the bathroom after Jeff, thinking about the stacks of Killians next to me.

"He's real close…real, real close," Benjamin, wearing a sombrero, said.

"What the hell? Is that you, Benjamin?" I asked.

"No, I' m Juan. Of course it's Benjamin. Keep your eyes open because Larry is very close by."

"Yeah, right. I'll find him tomorrow. Now I'm hanging out with my friends."

"He's here, he is here." The bathroom door opened and Benjamin was gone.

"See you in a minute," I said to Jeff as he headed to buy the beer.

"Don't stay in here too long…Larry's here right now and he could be leaving soon," said Benjamin as I almost peed on the wall when he once again startled me.

"Okay, okay. Just let me take a leak in peace for once."

***

The pair got in the car, drove to the convenience store and parked next to a little white 1987 Hyundai. A couple of guys were coming out of the store with cases of beer in their arms.

One bumped into Larry. "Excuse me, couldn't see how far my arms were sticking out. "

"That's alright," said Larry. "I should have been watching. They got quarts and six-packs here?"

"Yeah, we left you a few," said Wayne.

A couple of other guys were at the back of the car loading up a cooler. Larry got an idea. He and Vicky walked into the store, got a disposable Styrofoam cooler plus ice and a couple of six-packs (one Bud and one Lone Star) plus a quart of Mickey's malt liquor.

Larry overheard what seemed to be a familiar voice coming from the back seat of the Hyundai. When the person mentioned that he was looking for his long-lost brother, he imagined that it could be Jamie.

I got this strange feeling sitting in the back of Wayne's car that Benjamin was right. Even though I had looked at everybody in the store to see if they even slightly resembled him, it still felt like Larry was right there.

Chapter 33

Ronnie Meets Larry:

"Kid, for only being here a couple of days, you've really made an impression on folks hereabouts. I think it's safe to say that you're welcome back anytime," Duke said to Ronnie.

"You're sure you want to go to the big city, right? It's a big change from here," John added.

"Albuquerque's a small town compared to where I come from. You're not trying to welch on your deal, are you?" Ronnie said.

"Nope, *hasta mañana*, Duke. See you tomorrow. It's about a four-hour drive, son. *Vaminos*."

"Guess that means get in. Later, Duke, I'll stay in touch." Ronnie had said that many times before but he actually did mean it in Duke's case.

"We can take the more scenic drive through the Sangre de Cristo Mountains or go the quicker way via the interstate," John said as they got started up and buckled up.

"How much longer is the scenic route?"

"It could take up to six hours or a little less."

"Interstate, please."

The pair made their way along Highway 70 back to Raton and got on the interstate there headed for Albuquerque. The peaks of the

Sangres, a part of the southern Rockies, were on Ronnie's side of the Suburban.

Although it was only early October, a fresh dusting of snow could be seen atop the 11-12,000 foot peaks. When Ronnie saw the sign for Taos, he was a little enticed to get off of the freeway.

John could almost read his mind. "It's a nice drive over those mountains through Cimarron Canyon. Definitely worth it."

"We can just get off in a couple of miles. Let's do it. Who knows when I'll be back up this way?"

The road wended through the town of Cimarron then up into the canyon ever so slightly and into a deeper forest with tall trees. Route 64 crossed the Cimarron River in several places and there were signs to be careful of water on the road.

"That's mainly in the spring when there's a lot of runoff from melting snow," John said. "Hey, that guy looks like he needs some help with his car. Wanna' stop?"

"Not rea...," Ronnie said as John stomped on the brakes.

"Need some help?" John yelled to the driver of the 1963 Chevy truck.

"Just bought this damn thing and can't get it to stay in gear," he responded.

"It's your lucky day, we got a trannie expert right her," John said as he almost pushed Ronnie out of the car.

"Probably just the linkage. These old manual transmissions were known for that," Ronnie said. "Have you been underneath?"

"No, I don't know anything about these old trucks," the driver said.

Ronnie hopped underneath and readjusted the linkage in about two seconds. "Let me show you what I had to do. It's pretty simple."

"Get her fixed, Ronnie?" John asked. He had found out that the driver was going back to Albuquerque via Taos, unbeknownst to Ronnie.

"Yeah, we should be able to go in a second. Make sure it's working and I'll show you what to do," Ronnie said to the Chevy owner.

As they took off down the road, John followed them through every shift. When they stopped again, he said that the driver, Arturo, was going to take me the rest of the way.

"Our deal was that you take me in your comfortable Suburban. Not to put you down, Arturo. But I haven't ridden in anything this old since it was new."

"You'll be fine. Here you go, here's a few bucks to get yourself situated in the big city."

"Well, I guess this hundred bucks will come in handy. Give me my bag."

"Here you go, good luck."

"Don't worry, I can get you a job with mi amigo in 'Buerque at Manuel Transmissions," Arturo said.

The pair went through the mountains past shimmering Eagle Nest Lake, then spectacular Angel Fire and finally coming to the scenic but stoplight-dotted Taos. The ride had been relatively quiet but Arturo said he had to make a quick stop in town and Ronnie couldn't accompany him.

"I'll just drop you off at the plaza here and be back in a few minutes," Arturo said as he handed his passenger his duffel. "There are always some interesting characters here like in a lot of these artsy places."

Ronnie sat on the bench looking around for a few minutes. There were some Indians selling artwork on the edge of the park one way and a lady painting the scene on an easel in another corner.

"Passing through from Trinidad?" the passerby asked Ronnie.

"Huh, what?" Ronnie figured he looked pretty masculine now and was totally caught off guard that someone might have thought he'd had the sex change. Did every one around here have a sixth sense for telling that? "What makes you think that. Isn't that where they do all those operations?"

"What operations. That cardboard sign next to you says 'Trinidad bound, then 'Buerque' Isn't that your sign?"

"Oh. No, it's not."

Arturo pulled up and Ronnie got in the old truck. "Found someone to talk to right away, no?"

"Yes, I did. But can't wait to leave. Get your errand done?"

"Sure enough did."

The pair soon left Taos and went up into the mountains before hitting the road that ran alongside the northern Rio Grande. Ronnie just took in the sights until the Chevy got to Española.

"What's with those cars bouncing all over the place. Some are only a couple of inches from the ground?"

"Those are lowriders. They spend a lot of money to put hydraulics in them so they can hop like that and not bottom out. This is the world capital for them."

"Wow, that's crazy and they use a lot of old cars."

"This ain't New Yawk. Cars don't get old here."

It was about another hour and a half to Albuquerque and Arturo remained quiet until the pair got into the city. "Here's my buddy's tranny shop and there's a few motels right near by."

"Let's just stop here. It looks relatively clean."

"Yeah, the Zia Lodge is one of those old Route 66 motels which has managed to stay open. It's as good as any."

"Can you wait outside 'til I get a room? I'll tell you the number so you can pick me up and introduce me at your friend's shop tomorrow maybe."

"Yeah, that's cool."

Ronnie walked in, registered and got a key for room number 12. He couldn't help noticing that a Larry Goodman had also registered in the next room.

"Nah, it can't be. No way that's Jim's brother."

He yelled out the door to Arturo, "Room 12."

"*Bueno*, I'll call you in the morning."

Ronnie started walking to his room and saw a tall, blondish mid-twentiess man come out of his room with an ice bucket in one hand and a Lone Star beer in the other.

"Bet that stuff tastes like crap when it's warm," Ronnie said to him.

"It isn't even that great when it's cold but live and learn." Larry turned to face Ronnie as he spoke and the resemblance to Jim was subtle but there nonetheless.

Ronnie had to ask, "Do you have a brother named Jim, you look a lot like a guy I know?"

"My brothers are Jamie and Don. Last I saw them. It's been a few years."

Chapter 34

A Drug Deal Gone Good:

"Look, Wayne. I'll betcha that guy in the old Chevy truck is makin' a drug deal with the other guy. And I just saw some money drop," I said to my friend, who was giving me a ride to the Dautel house. "Park here for a minute and wait for them to leave. I'll split whatever I get with you."

"Who does a drug deal at six am? I gotta go to work. I've only got a...," Wayne was interrupted by me pointing to a bag being handed over.

"I'm sure they're not just recreational users. Someone needed a fix bad. It should only be a second. I'll get out as soon as they take off and walk nonchalantly over there; pretending like I dropped something while I scoop up the *dinero*."

They took off and I picked up a piece of white paper on my way over. I opened it up before dropping it as a decoy and then read my original name "Jamie Goodman" on it and saw "Larry Goodman at Zia Motor Lodge, Room 11."

I was in enough shock that I almost forgot to pick up the $125 in the middle of the parking lot. Luckily, nobody noticed.

"Steak dinner tonight. Found 125.dollars so we get 60 bucks each. Flip you for the extra five."

"Nah, you found it."

"Alright, let's go before they come back."

We drove a couple of blocks to 2801 Monroe and I showed Wayne the scrap with my name and my brother's on it. "I wouldn't be surprised if it came from Jack's house and blew down the street."

"I guess it's worth calling or going over there. Let me know what happens."

"Yeah, thanks for the ride, man. Talk at you later." I handed him his cut and got out in front of Jack's house.

Jack's wife Linda was the only one awake and I could smell the breakfast rolls with cheese and school lunches she was readying for the kids. I knocked on the door and looked in the kitchen window. She smiled when she saw me.

"Jimmy, how are you? How's things in Jersey (she was from there also)? What are you doing here so early?"

"Good. Jersey's still Jersey. It was the easiest time to get a ride. Want some help?"

"No, that's okay. You must be tired. Jack'll be up in a while. Go lay down and watch TV."

"Still making burritos for the snack wagon? I wouldn't mind having some chile. I sure did miss that. I'm not too tired to help with that."

"I'm sure you missed that. Let me start cooking and you can roll."

"Good deal. I'll get a contact high. Let me show you this piece of paper I found down the street. Think it might have blown off of your door."

She read it and turned a little pale. "You know, Cindy was asking me if I knew someone with some strange name. But now that I think about it, what she told me could have been Jamie Goodman."

"Maybe later on, I could try calling over there or even going to the motel with Jack when he gets up. Got a phone book. No wait, the note is on their letterhead with the number on it."

"I would wait a while, though. Only crazy people like us are up this early."

"I was planning on it." Cartoons came on the living room TV as I was wrapping the first ham, egg, potato and green chile burrito.

131

I walked in to the room and Cindy had made her way to the couch, the first step in awakening. "Hi, Uncle Jimmy, how aw you doing?" Cindy said from her prone position.

"I know you're still half awake but have you seen this piece of paper before?"

"Yeah, a man left it but I didn't know who he was talking about so I put it thewe, on the table. I asked my mommy the name and she didn't know it."

"Don't worry, you're not in trouble. Do you know what he looked like?"

"He was tawwer than Daddy with dirty bwonde haiw like Mommy's. He wooked a wittle wike you."

"Thanks, honey."

"I'm pretty sure it's him," I told Linda while re-entering the kitchen. I started rolling burritos again.

"You should just go over there with Jack when he gets up."

"Yeah, I guess after him being gone for ten years, anxiousness has set in."

***

Larry woke up to pee before he really woke up, as usually happened when he'd been drinking the night before. Hanging out with the clerk from the tramway had gone well into the wee hours and Larry went into Room 11's bathroom still half asleep.

"Don't go anywhere today, Jamie's coming," Benjamin said before Larry even had his zipper down.

"Piss on that," Larry said as he pulled back the shower curtain in search of the semi-recognizable voice. "Literally."

"No respect from you Goodman kids. I try to help my great-grandchildren and I just get pissed on. Every time."

"Ah, Benjamin, my perverted guardian angel, how the hell are you?"

"Never mind the formalities. Jamie, now calling himself Jim, is in town from New Jersey and he found your note. I'm so proud of myself. It was all because of me."

"Wait, he moved back east again and left this paradise. You knew that I was coming here a few days ago and –how come you didn't stop me then?"

"I thought that it might be too much of a shock for you to have to see everyone at the same time. I knew you were coming to find Jamie, hence the setup in New Mexico."

"Well, guess that makes some sense for your warped mind."

"Yeah and you should go back to sleep until later on; he probably won't show up until the afternoon."

"Sleep! How can I get back to sleep? We haven't seen each other in thirteen years when I was still a nerd who was shorter than him."

"Well then, you should just drive over there. Leave me here and I'll take care of Victor/Victoria when she wakes up."

"Sure, I know you'll take care of her. You still going for the Christine Jorgenson type, huh?"

"Old habits die hard."

"So do old guardian angels."

The phone rang and Larry knew that Vicky was probably was a little hung over. He jumped out of the bathroom and leaped onto the phone before it rang a second time.

"Hello."

"Front desk. Too early to send a call through?"

"Wait, so you're calling the room to make sure you won't wake anyone up when the phone rings?"

"Well, sir, when you put it that way it sounds stupid."

"Maybe that's because it is. Put the damn call through."

"Sorry. They hung up."

Chapter 35

Lost and Found:

"Who was that? What time is it?" Victoria mumbled, still half-drunk.

"It was the front desk but I think Jamie was trying to call. Go back to sleep."

She was already back asleep before he had answered. Maybe passed out was a better description.

Larry got the keys to the rental car and jumped in, intent on driving to 2801 Monroe. Then he realized that he needed directions. And he didn't trust the desk clerk.

"I'll just drive to the nearest gas station and ask," he said to nobody.

He drove a few blocks in what he thought was the right direction and espied an old Chevy truck with a guy underneath it. "Need some help? You know how to get to 2801 Monroe NE?"

"Nah, I got it. Yeah just take a left here, go over I-40 and look for Menaul, where you'll take a left. Then take a right on Monroe a few blocks up," Arturo said.

"Thanks, buddy."

Larry found a pack of Newports on the seat. "Ooh shit, Vicky's cigarettes, I'd better take them back 'cause she'll be pissed if she doesn't have one when she wakes up."

134

"Hey, Jack, can I borrow your car? I think that my brother is at the Zia Lodge. Don't ask how I know that."

Jack had just awoken. "What'd you sleep here last night?"

"No, Wayne gave me a ride before work. But, look, I found this piece of paper down the street."

"What's it say? I don't know where my glasses are."

"It's a note to Jamie Goodman from his brother Larry on Zia Lodge stationery."

"Here, take the wagon." He handed me the keys.

"Thanks, I'll put some gas; here's the snack wagon keys back in case I don't make it back on time."

"Okay. See you later, pal."

***

Larry had gotten a little lost going back to the motel but I knew right where I was going. So the timing was pretty close as Larry was headed back to the car while talking to Ronnie just as I pulled up.

And the '62 Chevrolet truck from earlier pulled up next to me. "Ooh, shit. I wonder if he saw me pick up that money in the parking lot," I said to myself.

"Hey, Arturo. I wasn't sure you'd show," said Ronnie who then saw me. "Jim, how crazy is this!"

"Ronnie...Larry. Wait, who is Arturo? Wait, Larry...Lawrence Jon Goodman?" I screamed like I hadn't since my mom died.

***

I told my Mom about the basketball game; how I had scored twenty points including a shot at the buzzer to win the game.

"Aren't you excited about that?"

"I just did what the coach asked me to do. I'm going to lay down."

"Don't you want to go celebrate?"

"No, I'm just really tired."

"How can you be so matter of fact about everything from winning the spelling bee to your first home run? I just don't get it."

"I don't know." I headed off to my room and laid down.

"Jamie, is that you?" my long-lost brother said. I had gone through years of correcting relatives that my name was Jim since I had thought Jamie to be effeminate. But I was not worried about that now.

"Yeah, it's me. We've got some catching up to do," I said as I hugged him. "Good to see you, Ronnie. I'll catch up with you later."

Victoria poked her head out the door and lit a cigarette. "What's all the noise, er...is this Jamie?"

"What do you think?" Larry said to her as he held our heads together.

It was all that I could do not to cry at the culmination of my ten-year hunt. I had only cried once as an adult and that was also when my Mom died. I'd been ready to call her for the first time in seven years and tell her that I was sorry even though I felt like I'd done nothing wrong. But fate had intervened and I never got to do it in time.

"I'm going to get ready so you guys can come in here and talk," Victoria said.

"That's okay, we'll just take a drive," Larry told her. "We'll be back in a couple of hours."

"I know some nice, quiet places in the mountains where we can talk. But I guess it's a bit early for a beer, how about a breakfast burrito?"

"Sounds good but you probably eat them spicy"

"Don't worry, we'll have them put the chile on the side. I'm a little out of practice with hot food since I've been back east a couple of years helping Dad."

Chapter 36

Reunion:

"Who would have thought that 'it's too early for a beer, how about a breakfast burrito?' would have been our first words to each other in thirteen years," I said to Larry as we headed on Route 66 towards Carnuel. I knew a little spot just east of Albuquerque where a small waterfall was only a short hike along a canyon stream.

"What do you mean? It's the perfect story to be telling our grandkids in thirty or forty years."

I still wasn't thinking of Larry as the twenty-six-year-old who'd led a life that must have taken some turns over the last decade. I still saw the nerdy thirteen-year-old who was collecting coins and ravenously reading World War II books until he'd become an expert in both subjects. But most of all, I couldn't believe that he was a Pittsburgh Steeler fan.

"So, I know that I missed a lot of your life but I really feel like you truly lacked guidance in your choice of pro football teams. Did you ever make it to the '79 Super Bowl? Last anyone heard was that you were headed to Miami for the game between two of my least favorite teams."

"Yeah, I made it. Even got a ride in the Goodyear Blimp. What's so bad about the Steelers. They were doing better than your Jets then and still are now?"

I commented on the Steelers playing dirty but not as much as the Raiders. But at least neither one of us liked the Cowboys.

"Yeah, one thing we can agree on; hating 'America's Team'. Anyway, I made it to the game using my thumb and I used my birthday money to get a ticket from a scalper. The game wasn't as popular back then and the prices weren't as high."

"But you were?"

"Were what?"

"High. You indulged in a little weed back then, I read in your diary. And maybe some other drugs, too."

"Yeah, I experimented but now the occasional joint is all that we do."

"We meaning that lady at the motel? She's a little older than you, huh?"

"Yeah, but I don't think you'd be seeing me alive today if it weren't for her. I wasn't ready to go home after the Super Bowl. I wasn't really ready for anything that life had to offer so I went to a beach that was closed due to sharks. And I took a bottle of Quaaludes with me intending to lay down at low tide after downing them."

"So you really were going to try to kill yourself. That's what Don always thought happened."

"You mean that I went through with it? Well, I would have if not for Vicky."

"The woman at the hotel?"

"Yeah, I was intending to OD and then have the high tide drag me out when it came until the sharks ate me. But Vicky, there on vacation from Greyhound, tackled me after talking for a few minutes."

"So she talked you out of it?"

"Well, sort of. She called me a chicken shit for not just wanting to jump in with the sharks and drown myself without using the pills. I

138

called her bluff and went to walk into the water but she wrestled me to the ground and saved me."

"Wow, that's crazy. What happened next?"

"I don't really know, conked my head on a conch after a shark tried to bite me. He only got my finger. Oh, and the bottle of 'ludes. They found a few passed-out sharks after high tide a few hours later."

"They must have had fun their last couple of hours cause sharks die if they can't swim. Or after a few minutes, at least"

I was thinking about the time I did a 714 at a club, think it was Alfalfa's on Lomas, once and the night of fun it led to with Janie or Gerry, maybe it was Joanie. Ah, can't remember her name but I was drinking that night, too.

"Yeah, woke up in the hospital with amnesia. Or so I'm told. And a nasty little wound on my finger." Larry showed me the scar and lack of mobility in his right index finger. But he was still able to use his middle finger and did so.

"Pretty funny, little brother. So you couldn't remember anyone?"

"Yeah, but Vicky was visiting me in the hospital and she told me that I was her boyfriend. And that the Pinecrest Lodge had given me a free room since we had cleared the sharks out and gotten the beach reopened. I believed her. It took me until 1982 to figure out my past and I tried to call Dad; he was still living in Fort Lee then. But I got mugged by some panhandler just before Dad accepted the collect call."

"Yeah, I heard about that call and there was screaming in the background. Everyone thought you had been kidnapped by the Moonies or some other cult."

Chapter 37

Taking Credit:

The conversation went on for a while with brothers rehashing everything from raccoon invasions during family vacations to Don and myself hitting Larry in the back in order to make him stop talking. The long-separated siblings were becoming so in sync that we even had to take a leak at the same time.

When we returned from the woods and got back in the car, I had an admission to make to Larry. "You know, I felt guilty when you took off and continued those feelings until this morning. Even though Mom wasn't allowing me to visit, I should have found a way to see you more often. Me and Don."

"Don was around plenty and I was going to do what I was going to do no matter what. My life changed a lot when Mom and Dad split up."

"Aw, isn't that cute! The two brothers making up for lost time and it's all because I got them together," Benjamin said from the back seat.

"Well, at least you didn't show up while I was peeing," Larry and I said in stereo.

"But the problem is that he showed up at all. Get out, Benjamin," I said emphatically.

"Second that," Larry said. "Come back later, give us a little time."

"Look at all the time I gave you. That's the gratitude I get for putting you boys together."

"There's a cactus over there with your name on it, Benjamin. While I'm grateful for your role in us reuniting, there's a prickly pear with one prick's name on it. Let's get him, Larry."

We got Benjamin to leave as Larry turned around in the passenger seat and kept him busy while I attacked from the left rear door. "I can take a hint. Be back later," Benjamin yelled as he was passing into his other dimension.

"I guess his crappy serape wouldn't protect him. Should let Jack know things are okay with his car. Take a ride with me? I know he will want to meet you."

"Yeah, but Vicky should be ready and we can follow you to Jack's house so that we can take off again. She'll want to meet you, too."

"Sounds good, by then it will be past noon so I can have my first beer with my little brother."

***

I remembered taking Larry for his first ride in my first car. The '68 Charger. He was still pretty nerdy at age eleven and he hadn't appreciate my revving the engine or speeding just to impress the local girls.

"Let's go home, Jamie" he said.

"Aw, come on. Someday you'll understand; hey, why don't we go to that deserted parking lot and I'll let you drive a little. And that's Jim, not Jamie."

"But I'm not old enough. I'll get in trouble."

"You can just tell them that I forced you if anyone says anything. I'm a lot bigger than you. It's either that or I go get a six-pack of Rolling Rocks and drink them while I'm driving."

"You're not old enough to buy beer. You can't do that."

"Why do you think I have this beard? I haven't been asked for ID in a couple of years."

"I suppose you smoke, too."

"Not cigarettes. But, in my defense, I sell a lot more weed than I smoke."

"Take me home so I can check out my coin collection. Right now!"

"Alright, let me just get a six-pack. I'll go hang out with my friends at the Old Mill."

Ah, the Old Mill in Woodcliff Lake, NJ. I met Rubin, Pickle and Ricky there. It was the town pool. We had keggers on the pavilion and went late night skinny dipping with Kim and a few other people.

I didn't realize that one night I'd be looking into my future when one of the guys who'd gone with us told us he was born with only one testicle. Despite the beautiful women with us, I couldn't stop staring at him little knowing that the crystal ball could have shown me that I'd lose one of my balls during my cancer a few years later.

***

"Jamie, Jamie!!! Are you hearing me? I think we have to turn here to get back to the motel."

"Oh, yeah. Just thinking back to your first ride in my Charger. Remember it?"

"Yeah, but I'm living in the here and now. A lot of shit happened in my past but I'd prefer to only remember the good times. Not when you tried to scare me by leaving rubber."

"Sure, you probably left brown racing stripes in your Fruit of the Looms that day. But you must have changed, more than your underwear, before high school since you decided to play football."

"Yeah, Mom was trying to keep me out of trouble since I didn't have a male role model. I ended up doing okay with it."

"Yeah, Don told me that you returned your first kickoff for a touchdown. I have mixed emotions since I always wanted to play football, even worked out with the team in the weight room. But Mom and Dad would never let me."

"I would gladly have traded playing football for living in the house instead of that shitty apartment. But it was fun, probably the only fun that I had back then without getting high."

Chapter 38

Of Ice Cream Truck Memories:

Turning into the Zia, I could see that Vicky was looking out the window. Larry got out and made his way back up to the beautiful old Route 66 motel. It was done in Art-deco and had the sign of the Zia Indians, also used by the state of New Mexico on its flag. The state lost a lawsuit a few years later for misappropriating the tribe's symbol.

The Zia symbol represents the sun with its rays radiating out in four directions. With over three-hundred days of sun per year, New Mexico was the original "Sunshine State" before Florida borrowed that name.

"Does it ever rain here? I haven't even seen a cloud in the three days we've been here," Larry said when he came back out. Vicky was right behind. "Oh, Jamie...er...Jim, this is Vicky."

I noticed her hands were a little oversized but didn't think too much of it. "Nice to meet you, Vicky."

"So Larry said you took him to some small waterfalls. Where does the water come from?"

"Oh, it still rains in the mountains at night sometimes. Shall we split to Jack's house. You're following me, right?"

"Yes, brother. Mind if I call you that until I get used to calling you Jim?"

"No problem, just don't call me Brother Jim. Some people will think that I'm part of a church. Definitely don't want that."

We got into our respective vehicles and drove up Washington where some of the nicest homes in Albuquerque were at the time. It wasn't long until we were at the Dautel home in a more modest neighborhood.

"Did you see that house with seven garages on it? That's a Kennedy family home." I said to my brother and Vicky as they exited the car.

I knew how to get to a lot of places but the only ones I researched were the bars. There was a time when I could say I'd been to every bar, tavern or saloon in Albuquerque.

"Yeah, I noticed; pretty nice place," Larry said.

I turned the front door knob to go inside. "You're not going to knock first?" Vicky asked.

"No, I'm always welcome here." As I walked in, a Jedi light saber flew past my head. "Well, almost always."

"Sorry, Uncle Jimmy," Annie and Cindy said in unison.

Jack and Linda were in the kitchen with the snack wagon having done its morning and lunch runs.

"Wow, he looks like you," Linda said.

"Poor son of a bitch," Jack joked.

"I never thought that I'd be saying this but this is my brother Larry and his girlfriend Vicky... Jack and Linda Dautel."

"And I never thought that I'd be seeing him again," Jack said. "Do you remember the last time you saw me, Larry?"

"Gotta' say, I don't. A lot of things have happened in the past ten years," Larry said.

"I'll give you a hint. It was at George White School," Jack said.

Larry looked at him up and down. Jack was a great guy but dressing well was not one of his fortes. Vanity was a four-letter word to me as well.

"Don't think you were a teacher or a principal. Did you offer candy to little girls in the schoolyard with Jamie?" Larry said with a smile directed my way.

"Well, Ja-mie sold the illegal candy but I actually did sell candy to girls…and boys."

"Don't you start calling me Jamie now too!"

144

"Oh, wait! Dd you have the ice cream truck when I was in eighth grade at George White?"

"Yeah, my parents were there more often but I came to help sometimes."

"Oh, yeah. I used to con them out of ice creams talking…"

"They let you think you were conning them but your brother was actually paying for your frozen desserts. Ja-mie was a good brother."

"Stop calling him Jamie. You know he doesn't like it," Linda said.

"Aah, it's alright for now. Thanks though, Linda-I'll live."

"They were nice old people, your parents. How are they doing now?"

"Actually, they passed away in '86," Jack said.

"That's too bad," Vicky said.

"Yeah, there wasn't too much good going on in my life then. I had fun with your parents. Dad had already moved out and he was fighting with Mom whenever they were together and Don, he was hardly ever there. Jamie…er…Jim couldn't come by after his trouble with Mom but he was around sometimes. I had a friend named Al Moss and a few other people at school but pretty much was alone when I came home."

"I'm going to get going, Larry. I'm tired. Just call me if you want a ride home in a while," Vicky said as she was leaving.

Chapter 39

Secrets Exposed:

"Everything came through just like I said it would, didn't it?" Benjamin, still sporting the sombrero and serape, asked.

Vicky, shocked at his appearance in the car, was speechless. But she also knew exactly why he was there.

"I made good on my word. Now how about we keep things status quo?"

"Well, yeah…Larry got together with his family. But we got really close on this trip. I'd feel guilty if he found out about us."

"I can help with things going smooth for Larry in the future. That is if you make things go smooth for me. I haven't been able to find anyone to satisfy my needs here yet."

"Have you even been trying? I can see that there are plenty of hookers near the fairgrounds and further east...surely someone's got to know a tr…."

"Why do I want to work so hard when everything that I need is right here?" Benjamin caressed and moved up Vicky's thigh with a touch that Larry could never even aspire to have.

Vicky responded immediately and could barely get the motel room door open in time. "You suck!" she yelled at Benjamin.

"I know and I've been trying to teach you but you're still not as good as me." He was back to looking like a lecherous, old Jewish guy once he removed the Mexican garb.

***

"Something is telling me that I should go back to the motel," Larry said. "Jim, can you give me a ride in a few minutes?"

"As long as Jack doesn't need the car."

"Well, I do have to run a few errands this afternoon. But I could give you guys a ride over there."

"I can just call Vicky. She should be awake by now."

***

Benjamin was just finishing up when the phone rang in the room. With her mind in other places, Vicky didn't even hear it until the fifth ring

"I'd better get that. It might be Larry."

"All the more reason not to get it."

"No, I have to. He might need a ride." She picked up just in time to hear a dial tone.

***

"Guess she's still sleeping," Larry said as he hung up the old rotary wall phone at Jack's house. "Yeah, maybe you could give me a ride."

"Sure, we just have to make one quick stop along the way," Jack said. He was a great friend but was always business first. At age forty-four, he still hadn't ever taken a vacation.

I knew he was wanting to stop at an auto parts store for either the snack wagon or one of the myriad vehicles he was fixing up to resell. No big deal, beggars can't be choosers.

We took Boomer with us, too. Jack's son went everywhere with him as long as he wasn't in school. He offered me the front seat.

"That's okay. I'll sit in back with my brother."

We drove, literally two minutes to APK Auto Parts on Menaul.

"I don't know if we could fit a bumper in this car with the four of us." I remembered a few times returning from the flea market having to

147

hold things on the roof or out the windows as they were too big for Jack's economical vehicles.

"No worries, it's just a tune-up kit for the truck."

He was back out in a minute and we were almost there when it happened...a yard sale sign. "Let's drive by real quick. It's probably just clothes anyway," Jack said.

"Can you just drop us off here? I'm not up for looking through buckets of tools right now," I said.

"You sure? C'mon, we'll just go real quick to check it out. I'll even stop calling you Jamie."

"Yeah, let's go Jimmy," Boomer said.

"Larry?"

"Ah, what the hell. maybe we'll find some souvenirs."

A half-hour later, we were still at the yard sale with Jack making a pile of tools he was going to buy and me arguing with Larry about some fake turquoise.

"Watch, if you heat the end of a safety pin and stick it in the stone, you'll see it pierce through. Proving that it's not turquoise." I was getting a dirty look from the garage sale's proprietress.

"I don't care. It looks nice and Vicky would like it. It's only 10 bucks."

"Larry, if you still want to buy it now, at least you'll be making an informed decision."

"Good, so you'll loan me the ten dollars then. Vicky will give it back to you."

"Wow, that's pretty nice. You're buying her a present with her money."

Smiling, Larry said, "It's the thought that counts, right?"

Jack was paying twenty-six dollars for a big pile of tools and Larry got his authentic turquoise-colored plastic ring. Jack already had stuff in the trunk so some of the tools shared the back seat with Larry and I.

"At least it's only a short ride, Jack," I said with a breaker bar lying across my lap.

We got to the motel a minute later. "Hey, look at that crazy tourist with a serape and sombrero walking by the ice machine. He must think he's in Mexico. We should tell him that he can still get dysentery from the ice," I said. The guy walked around the corner and disappeared.

"You can just let us off here," Larry said. "Thanks for the ride. Wait out here while I check to make sure Vicky's awake, Jim."

Chapter 40

Back on the Bus:

"Jaa-cob, you're back already," Victoria said, half asleep from under the blanket, as Larry opened the door to room 12.

Larry wasn't sure he'd heard her muffled voice correctly. "Yeah, it's me and I brought Jamie along. He's still outside."

"Uh, alright. I'll get up in a minute."

"I'll wait outside with my brother. Man, I like the sound of that."

Vicky got up and took a quick scan of the room to make sure Benjamin hadn't left anything behind. She got into the shower after she was confident there was nothing.

"What are you doing taking a shower again? It's the middle of the day," Larry yelled to her.

"Trying to wake up. Sorry, it must be the altitude."

Larry sat down on the bed and pulled the ring he had just bought out of his pocket. He was looking at the floor near the door when...

"Arggh...Benjamin. That's you again under that sombrero?"

"Fits better than a yarmulke. Do you like the poncho to go with it?" Always one step ahead, Benjamin had changed outfits but stayed with the Mexican motif.

"Your mother would be proud. What's going on?"

"Jim's outside waiting...don't you think you should invite him in? Or at least hang out with him until Vicky gets out of the shower?"

"I suppose so." Larry went outside and with one fell swoop Benjamin picked the ring up off of the floor which he had dropped in his haste while leaving a few moments ago. He went to visit Vicky in the shower.

"Benjamin, get out of here. What are you doing with Larry right out there?"

"He's outside. Hold on, my poncho's getting wet. Damned Sears poncho!"

With one touch, all Victoria's protests ended. But Benjamin was cut short when the door slammed.

"Vicky, you almost done?"

"Be right out!" She had wanted to finish what Benjamin started but now could not without making Larry suspicious.

"What were you masturbating in there?" Larry said as Vicky came out of the shower.

"No, sorry. I just couldn't wake up."

"Here, I got you this ring. Like it?"

Victoria's eyes opened wide. It was the same ring as Benjamin had been wearing earlier. "W-where did you find that?"

"At a yard sale around the corner. What's wrong with you? Don't you like it?"

"N-no, it's nice. I'll be ready in a second."

"That's cool. I just have to go to the bathroom." Larry walked in and did his business but when he turned around to wash his hands, he looked at the ring on the floor. "How did that get in here?"

Upon further examination, Larry found that the ring was a man's ring although a duplicate of the one he'd just purchased. Except for the JH monogram etched inside.

"Benjamin Epstein, that son of a bitch fake guardian angel mother fuckin' fairy great-grandfather. I knew he couldn't leave Vicky alone."

**

Like all three Goodman boys, Larry didn't like to argue. He had seen too much arguing between his parents while growing up. They

151

managed to stay together for thirty-three years but that may have been about twenty-five years too long.

Larry entered the room holding the ring. "Look at this ring. I wonder how it got into the bathroom and got JH etched into it. You just couldn't keep away from that guy, could you?"

"What can I say? I'm sorry, so sorry. Please give me another chance. I promise to stay away from him."

"Yeah, you've promised that before. I think it's time for us to make a decision. I'm not going to tell you where to live but I can tell you that it's not going to be with me."

"B-but I did it for you...he promised to get you back together with your family." Vicky was crying.

"Whatever he promised has already come true. It would have happened with or without him. Do you want to stay here or are you gonna go back east again?"

"I-I'll stay here, I g-guess." She was hoping that Larry would change his mind. He had relented about Benjamin hanging around upon first finding out about their previous affair.

"Don't think I'm going to change my mind this time. If you stay here, nobody is coming around. Especially not me."

She could see that Larry meant what he said. Vicky was back on the bus the next day. At least she got to travel for free and could always come back if Larry asked her to.

Chapter 41

Havin' a Beer or two:

"You doin' okay, kid?" I asked Larry after Victoria had left us alone at the motel.

"As good as could be, I guess. I-I just don't know if I was meant to have any permanent relationships in my life. Family or otherwise."

"Yeah, I've felt the same way before. Somehow I usually find a way to fuck things up. Starting with mom and following me through my twenties. I'm gonna' call Wayne up. That negative sonuvabitch can make anyone else's life look good."

Wayne might be negative but he was dependable. He was happy that I'd found my brother and wanted to meet him. Larry went to use the bathroom while I called Wayne and he offered to let me use his car the next day.

"I'll turn you into a fairy godmother you lying, cheatin' sonuvabitch."

"Oh, goody. Benjamin's back," I said to myself. It sounded like Larry was ready to give his great-grandfather a bilateral orchiectomy. I know that term because I had one of my nuts removed (a unilateral) to cure my testicular cancer in 1986. It didn't sound like Larry had created a sterile field to perform the operation.

153

"Now calm down. I got you together with your brother, didn't I?" Benjamin's serape had a small rip at the bottom from Larry's stiletto. "I swear I get no gratitude from these kids. I'm going to go find Vicky."

"Go to Vicky, go. You two deserve each other. Get the fuck out of my sight before I turn your groin into granola!"

Benjamin appeared to me in the other room. "I'd better get out of here. Larry's pretty mad. At least his brother, with more common sense, isn't mad at me too."

I took the lamp and tried to jam it between Benjamin's legs. "Yeah, you light up my life. I don't think New Mexico is a good place for you!"

"That's the problem with this generation. You all feel entitled to help from good people like me. You should have seen the Great Depression…"

"You're gonna' have a great depression in your head and between your legs if you don't take off right now."

"I just don't get it, just don't get it," Benjamin said as he and his sombrero faded into the sunset.

"And take your fuckin' ring," I yelled as it made its way toward the door via Air Jim.

Wayne pulled up a couple of minutes later in his Hyundai. I was waiting for him and half-watching for my fairy godfather to return.

"My brother's inside and yeah, fuck you, he's skinnier than me."

"Well that ain't saying much. Got a beer?"

"Might be one inside." I held the door open and introduced Wayne.

"Well, your brother is better looking than you. But that ain't saying much either. Got a beer?"

"There should still be a couple in the fridge. Let me look," Larry said.

There were only three Lone Stars left and Wayne was a Budweiser guy. Unless there was nothing else. Then he was just a beer guy.

"This will do for now but we'll have to go get some more soon," I said.

"Yeah, the first one always tastes okay but the second east Texas beer tastes like west Texas smells. We need some Budweisers!"

"See, Larry. Told you how he was. But down deep he ain't bad. Sometimes it takes a while to peel back the layers. Wayne's from Long Island, too. Islip."

"Well, I was born in Bethpage at Mid-Island Hospital and lived in Massapequa; Plainedge to be exact until '71 when we moved to Jersey. My brothers remember more about the Island than I do since I was only eight when we left."

"But you remember Jones Beach and Lollypop Farm; places like that, right?"

"We saw the big turtle at that farm and went to the beach a lot. I fell out of the car on the way back from there once, I heard," Larry said.

"Yeah, you were good at falling on your head...did it through the basement window well once too," I said.

Wayne let me borrow his car to get more beer and, in the meantime, he and Larry got to know each other. And Larry still wanted to get to know Coors, which still left a sour taste in my mouth especially after it was boycotted in New Mexico due to their Hispanic hiring and employment practices.

It wasn't long after I'd gotten to New Mexico that there were blockades on all the border crossings from Colorado stopping all the Coors trucks and turning them around. I remembered seeing one between Aztec and Durango. Pretty scary stuff. Even the ones I saw on the news.

"I'm back," I said making sure that Wayne saw the six-pack of Coors purchased for Larry.

"I know you've got fuckin' Budweiser outside or I ain't givin' you no ride no where, no how."

"C'mon. Try it, you'll like it."

"I think I like your brother better than you. I don't wanna have to get up unless it's to piss out some rented Budweiser."

155

"Calm down. I just wanted Larry to taste the Coors." I got a case of Bud out of the car which wouldn't all fit in the fridge. "Time to head for the ice machine. I'm gonna use your cooler."

"No Coors touches that cooler though!"

"No problem." I gave Larry a Coors and Wayne a Bud before getting the ice bucket and heading out the door. I heard somebody spew their beer.

"Think I'd rather have a Bud," Larry said.

"Likin' your brother a lot better than you."

"No big loss," I said. "I'll trade you in on a friend with two good ears."

Chapter 42

Getting Larry Home:

We took off in Wayne's car and my wheels were spinning about how to get Larry back to the rest of the family. So I just asked Wayne, "Driving to New York anytime soon?"

"Not planning on it. Why?"

"Trying to figure out how to get Larry back east." Central Avenue on the east side of Albuquerque had a seedy character what with its shattered windows and shattered lives along the street. But there was good food in what we knew as the War Zone.

The flavors were mostly Mexican and New Mexican but something new had been added in the early eighties when a lot of the boat people had settled here. That meant Vietnamese restaurants and even a Buddhist temple. Vietnamese restaurants were cheaper than the Chinese variety with at least the same quality. Sometimes better.

"Hey, y'all hungry. Let's stop here and grab a bite." I had been to Pho Nguyen previously and liked it, besides they had no forks or spoons there.

"Y'all...that cracks me up...you're really from back East? I've never had Vietnamese before," Larry said. "Sounds good to me."

"They have beer? ...er... Budweiser?" Wayne asked. He didn't realize how much he would need some in a few minutes.

"Yup. They have Bud." Wayne screeched on the brakes and we were inside, beers in hand and ordering, within a minute.

Our soups came with the ladle-like utensils often used in Oriental restaurants and chopsticks were placed all around. Our food arrived a beer later. Wayne asked the waitress for a fork.

"Thank you. No fork," said the server.

"Well, guess you get to eat with chopsticks again," I said to Wayne. Holding my chopsticks was easier than holding back a grin.

"Very funny," he said as he soaked the utensils in his water. It was his feeble attempt to make them grip better.

Wayne's mother hadn't required him to eat his spaghetti with chopsticks as ours had with lo mein. Larry and I weren't missing a beat while my old friend was consistently missing his mouth.

"How's the food, Wayne?" I asked. "Need another beer to wash it down?"

"My shirt would be loving the food if I was your size, asshole," he said as another noodle slipped from between the sticks.

Even my proficiency with the Oriental utensils didn't stop me from getting some on my shirt. It was kind of like they said with the Romans how they burped after a good meal. Well, I did that too.

Larry, as opposed to Wayne, was totally enjoying his food. "It's like riding a bicycle, I'll bet I haven't used chopsticks in five years. I'm liking New Mexico."

"It's hard not to like it...great food and great weather, beautiful women and incredible scenery," I said. I couldn't wait to come back after a couple of years in New York again. "If only they had Genny Cream..."

"Ah, Genny Cream." Wayne seconded my opinion about Genesee Cream Ale, a beer from upstate New York which had a uniquely smooth flavor. I'd once brought back fifteen cases to New Mexico on a road trip for Wayne and Terry, another friend from Delaware. There was a time you could probably have made good money bringing Coors to New York and Genny Cream out west .on the return trip.

"Think I'll stay here. At least for a while," Larry said.

"But you do want to see Dad and Don; he has a son now? And Dad remarried. We have three stepsisters."

***

"Watch, Meri. You just hold the one like a pencil. It stays stationary while the other one you use to push against it and grab things," I said to my youngest stepsister. She was going to teach her class how to use chopsticks, at my suggestion.

She tried and dropped the chopsticks. I calmly picked them up and placed them in the right position so she could hold them. I knew it took some getting used to.

I felt like a big brother all over again when I was with he...she reminded me of my clumsiness at that age and I enjoyed giving her a ride or helping her here or there. I would really miss her when I moved back to New Mexico, which would be coming in the next couple of years.

But she was starting college and would have her own life by then.

When I had met Meri, she was thirteen—the same age Larry was when I had last seen him before yesterday. I picked him up and took him to my father's place in Fort Lee, where we stayed for a couple of days before I moved out west in 1976.

Wow, the same age Larry was. Hope I wasn't using Meri as a substitute for Larry. I got along with all three of my stepsisters but everyone said that my youngest stepsister and I seemed like we were on the same wavelength.

And I wanted it to stay that way.

***

"Jamie...er...Jim, come back to reality. You've only had two beers," Larry said.

"Oh...uh, sorry. I was just thinking about stuff."

"Yeah, your brother has a lot of flashbacks. I can't believe that he didn't do a lot of LSD when he was younger."

"What can I say. I'm just on a natural high."

159

"Ahhh, you're just naturally high. Someday, you'll write a book and kill yourself like Hemingway but I'll probably put myself out of my misery (from hanging out with you) first," Wayne said.

"Oh, yeah...here's a fork, fucker."

Larry was laughing. It was the first time I'd really seen that since Victoria had left. And I hadn't seen it enough in the last thirteen years to get used to it.

"Anyways, I'd like to stay here a while. If they want to come see me, they can come here."

"You know, Dad's already in his seventies and Don is married with a son. It's not as easy for them to travel as us."

"Yeah, but I have no money and I need to start my new life. I'd rather start it here."

Chapter 43

Hi, This is Larry:

"Hey, Dad. You sitting down? I ran into someone you might want to talk to," I had called my father from Jack's house. The yellow 1950's rotary wall phone in his kitchen had seen a lot of wear and heard a lot of stories since it'd been installed when the house was first built. I found out my mother had died and Jack found out about his parents moving west and many other things happened over the years.

But none quite like this.

"What's going on, Jim? Did you meet up with an old girlfriend and now you're not coming back to New York?"

"No, I'll be back but trust me! You want to sit down...Just trust me." Five years ago, my words might not have reassured him. But now that my father had been around me for a while, he let cooler heads prevail.

"Okay, okay. I'm sitting down."

"Hi Dad, this is La...," Larry was interrupted by our father.

"Oh, my God. Larry! I recognize your voice...I thought you were dead...I thought I'd never see you again. Where are you, New Mexico? Where have you been?"

"Yeah, I'm in Albuquerque with Jam...er, Jim. And there'll be plenty of time to answer all your questions. But I like it here and want to check it out for a while."

I was still standing next to Larry and it was obvious my father was choking back the tears on the other end of the line. "But, but…you're gonna come back here first and we'll all get together."

"No, I'm comfortable here for now. Can't you come here?"

"What if I get you some money...can you at least come up for a week or so?"

"I'm just getting used to my new life and I want to get a job and a place. A place of my own. I've never had that before."

"What have you been doing? How did you live. Were you homeless?"

"I'll answer all your questions but not now. I'm on Jim's friend's phone and they have four kids. I can't tie it up. Here's Jamie."

"Glad I told you to sit down, huh? I'm sure you didn't expect that voice."

"Hi Jim, Susan. Your father went to get a little Johnny Walker. You have to get Larry to come up here so everyone can meet him."

"Uh-oh, that's serious." I knew my father always kept the smoother black version of the blended scotch around but he hardly ever touched it. I might have gone for a single malt myself but maybe married people like blended better.

***

"Dad, put down the bottle. It's not that b..," I yelled as the half-empty bottle crashed against the top of the dresser.

"I'm a bad father, a bad provider. I've fucked up our whole world!"

My father didn't curse or drink often but things had come to a head that week after Don got busted at a Dead show in Passaic on Friday and took off only to get busted again the following night. That compounded the problems with my father's company bankruptcy and us losing the house in Hillsdale. Then there was the impending divorce.

"Let's think about this." All I was really thinking is why didn't he offer me some before he broke the half-empty bottle on my dresser. But I had to focus.

"You and Mom had thirty-plus great years and I've had eighteen. Donnie just took a couple of steps on the wrong path but look at how

162

good Larry is doing." I was pretty lucky to have never gotten caught doing anything worse than speeding considering how much pot I'd sold and how much electronics I'd helped boost out of cars.

"Larry, what's going to happen to Larry when we lose the house? How am I gonna afford a lawyer for Don? Where's everybody going to live? I don't want to live!!!"

"C'mon Dad, that's ridiculous," He raised the bottle's neck closer to his neck and I thought that I'd better do something. I broke my lava lamp (hated those stupid things anyway) and lifted it as if I was going to put it to my neck.

While my father's guard was down, I took the lamp and hit what was left of the bottle to shatter it in my father's hand. There was some blood but it was a quick way to avert a lot more blood.

***

"Jim, Jim!" One great thing about my stepmom and her family is that they had never known me as Jamie. But, on the downside, Susan could be relentless and quite persuasive if she thought that things should be a certain way.

"Yeah, Susan. I'll see what I can do but I'm not sure the chances are good." I knew that meant another phone call in a few days. "Alright, I'd better get off my friend's phone."

Goodbyes were exchanged but then I thought that reminding my father to call Don would be a good idea. I did so and yelled that I was off the phone. The scampering of little feet signaled that the kids had heard me.

Luckily, I had a pocketful of small change that I threw to keep them busy for a few minutes.

"Boy, don't think our family was ever like that. I'd really like to see Don too but I'm just not ready to go back over there," Larry said.

"I understand. Just take your time. I had to get away for seven years myself."

Chapter 44

You Can Drink the Water but the Beer's A Lot Better:

"You know, you don't need a damned passport to come here. I don't understand...you fly to Cancun every year. It isn't as far to come to Albuquerque," I told my father who had called on the Zia Lodge phone.

Larry would have to be checking out today so that number was safe to give out if I didn't want further calls discussing bringing Larry back to New York.

"Yeah, but Jim, everyone wants to see him from Don's wife to the girls to your cousins and aunts and uncles."

"I think what matters now is what he wants. You don't want to scare him off again, do you?"

Silence on the other end. I didn't really think Larry would take off again but it was a possibility.

"Alright, alright. I'll see what I can do to get away before you come back from vacation."

"Take your time a little, Dad. He might want to get settled in first anyways."

I called Larry to come talk on the phone and it turned out that Don was also with Dad waiting to talk to his younger brother.

"Little brother, is that really you?"

"Yeah, hi Don. It's been a long time."

"Wow, Dad was right. Your voice really is recognizable. I never thought that I would hear it again."

"Well, yeah, life was kinda messed up last time I saw you. But things changed."

"Yeah, when I read your diary, I really thought you might have jumped off a bridge somewhere."

"I actually did try to off myself but someone saved me. I'll tell you more when I see you."

"Yeah, I'm sure there's lots of blanks to fill in. We'll talk to you soon."

We started getting Larry's stuff together so he could get moved out. Nobody was too sure where exactly he was going. I knew Wayne or Jack didn't have room. But I wondered if Jack had a rental he was fixing up anywhere that Larry could stay at in trade for work. That would work perfect.

Larry had everything packed in five minutes but there was one thing we couldn't take with us. While Larry got his belongings into one suitcase, there were still two suitcases only partly full.

"Hey Wayne, we need some help. We got Larry packed up but there's two suitcases we couldn't take along," I said to Wayne on the phone.

"I need to stay home for a while with my son."

"The cases say Budweiser and Rolling Rock on them."

"Be right there. With little Wayne if you'll watch him."

"I c...," the phone clicked and Wayne was strapping his son into the car seat, I figured. He pulled up ten minutes later just as Ronnie was coming out of her...his room.

I was coming out to see Wayne when I heard Ronnie's voice. "Jim, how you doing?"

"How bad could it be when I just found my missing brother, Ronnie? What are you up to...got time for a beer?"

"Well, I'm getting ready to move into a place. Been working for a couple of days and my boss gave me a good deal. Yeah, I got time for one."

165

"Wayne, this is Ronnie Ferraro. He grew up in Plainedge, too."

"Actually, I'm Ronnie Ferraro Johnson. Jim, I didn't tell you that I added the Johnson on."

"What, oh, okay." All I could think about for the next ten minutes was how not to say that I knew Veronica had added a johnson to become Ronnie but hadn't known that he added Johnson to his name also.

A six-pack later, I was the only one who'd had only one beer. Wayne's two-year old was the only one more sober than me but Ronnie, that was another story. I was afraid he might spill the beans about his past life and Wayne Sr. wasn't ready for that. They had gotten to know each other the past little while but that part hadn't come out.

"You know, Larry, I'm gonna have some extra room at my place if you want. It's nothing fancy. Just a little apartment behind the transmission shop where I'm working."

"Can you spot me on the rent for a couple of weeks. I don't even have a job yet. And how much would it be?"

"Why don't you come see it and we'll figure things out? It would be cheap."

"Let's go check it out in three more beers. Just enough for each one of you," I said. It could never be disputed how much I like beer but I could have just as easily gone without it.

The baby was even catching the good vibes in that room when I realized that he hadn't cried in a while.

"How's the water in your place? I'm sure it's drinkable," Larry said.

"The water's good for showers, the beer's much better to drink," Ronnie said.

"You're learning about New Mexico quickly," Wayne said.

Chapter 45

As If I Needed Convincing to Stay:

We drove the couple of blocks to Ronnie's new place since he had his stuff with him and so did Larry. While certainly not extravagant, the apartment was livable and Larry wouldn't have to couch surf since there was a small second bedroom with a little room for my brother to even put a few decorations.

It didn't seem too noisy but then again, the transmission shop up front wasn't open on Sunday. Hopefully, Larry would have a job and not be there too often when the pneumatic tools were being used.

Drunk people are either really hard to deal with or really easy to deal with. Luckily, Larry and Ronnie both fell into the latter category and a deal was struck. There wasn't a separate meter for water, electric or gas on the apartment but Ronnie said his boss, Manuel, wouldn't charge for utilities if they used them conservatively.

We were walking out onto the street when I spotted a woman who looked vaguely familiar, walking with a six or seven-year-old boy. They looked like they had been down on their luck as many people did in this neighborhood.

"Jimbo, didn't that girl used to shoot darts? I know I recognize her," Wayne said.

"Yeah, now that you mention it, I think she did," I replied. "She had that twin sister. I remember going out with one and the other one tried to fool me."

"That's right, huh. Jackie…,"

"And Josie Chavez. Wonder which one she is?" The boy with her came into view and he reminded me of Larry at that age. "Jackie," I yelled to her.

"No, I'm Josie. Is that you, Jim…and Wayne?"

***

Bing, bang, boom. I had hit a ton twenty (120) out before but it never felt so good. I felt a real connection with the girl hugging me and it didn't hurt that we had won the doubles dart tournament at the Penguin Lounge that Thursday in 1982.

"Good shootin', Jim. You kicked ass with that out," Jackie said.

"Yeah, we make a good team. It wasn't all me." I said.

"We should go get some fresh air after we split the winnings." The fresh air wasn't really that fresh as it was dart shooter slang for marijuana. Whether I actually smoked or not, it wasn't as often as I would have liked that a beautiful woman asked me to go outside.

It was a good night and Joyce, who was running the tournament, gave us eighty-eight dollars to share plus the seven dollar bar tab that came with first place. The bar tab was actually worth more than the cash since the numbers could be changed and it could be used infinitely with the almost blind bartender.

We both finished our drinks and went outside before breaking in the new bar tab. When she asked me if I had any pot, I could see that she didn't really care whether we got high or not.

"I don't. You were the one who asked me to come outside."

"Oh well, yeah. I did." She kissed me, one thing led to another and we were in the back of my van. And we saw each other for a couple of weeks until her crazy sister fooled me into thinking that I was with Jackie.

Jackie got mad and said that I should have been able to tell the difference. And maybe I could have if I would have been a little more motivated to do so.

***

"Jamie, er… Jim. You with us? Did you hear what she just said? He does look like you," Larry said.

"Huh, what---who looks like me?"

"You didn't hear, did you? My son Jerry. I'm pretty sure he's your son too," Josie said.

"Huh…what…we were only together once. Otherwise me and Jackie would probably still be together."

"Oh, he's yours. Look at the little pot belly," Wayne said.

"And the bucked teeth and curly dirty blonde hair like you had at that age. I saw it in pictures," Larry was kind enough to point out.

"Let's not talk about this in front of Jerry…when can we get a blood test done, Josie? I'm only here on vacation so we should try to do it in the next few days."

Josie proceeded to throw a fit. "You've been out of his life all this time and all you can think about is a blood test. You son of a bitch!!"

"You could have found me when you were pregnant and I was still living here. But let's talk more and not in front of Jerry."

"You should just give me some money until we can get this damned test," Josie yelled. I felt sorry for her kid whether I was the father or not.

"I'll meet you at the restaurant down the street, Cocina de Carlotta, in a half hour and buy you all lunch." I took a twenty out of my pocket, tore it in half and gave it to her. "You can have the other half after we eat."

"Well, your family got a lot bigger this week between your brother and your son. He really does look like you at that age and have the same mannerisms," Ronnie said.

"We'll see…if it's true, it really has been quite a week."

Chapter 46

Things Change:

"You have a nice looking son; he looks just like his dad," the waitress said. "You can really tell he's your son."

"Thank you; he's quite a boy," I said. She was probably just looking for a tip but her comments were well-timed. For Josie.

"He even likes red chile just like his daddy," Josie said.

"I hadn't eaten chile yet when I was his age." I gave a little dirty look to Josie, being careful that Jerry didn't see me. We ordered enchiladas and a *gordita* for the budding *gordito* and it was all good. Especially the *sopaipillas*. Most people put honey on them, but Jerry (like me) used it to mop up the extra chile around the sides of his plate.

"Well, isn't that cute," said the waitress observing us trying to sop up the last of the savory sauce. She put her arm around Jerry and asked him if he wanted another *sopaipilla*.

"Yes, thank you," I said and she brought us two more. "So, when are we going to set up this test or, better yet, when are you going to be available so I can set it up? I'll pay for it."

"You REALLY need a damned test! He looks like you, acts like you and even eats like you. What other proof do you need?"

"I just want to be sure—especially after this week when my brother finally caught up with me after ten years of thinking I saw him. Thinking I found him. But I don't want to argue here."

"Mommy, that was good," Jerry said. "I like Uncle Jim, too."

"I'm glad, Jerry. Now wipe your mouth and go to the bathroom to clean up. You got a little rice on your shirt."

I looked down and my shirt had a stain in the exact same spot as Josie's son. Luckily it wasn't chile this time.

"Jerry's not here now and I want you to pay for your son. You've been absent for his first seven years. Don't you think you should be around to make up for lost time?"

"I want to, but I'm staying in New York for a while. Unless we take a blood test and it comes out positive."

"POSITIVE!! I'm already POSITIVE. How much more proof do you need?"

"I just want something scientific other than a bunch of coincidences. It's kind of like a jury convicting without corroborating evidence."

"He hears like you and he says things like you. The way you say huh even though you hear something and how he explains things like you do...no test is going to prove any more than that. He even daydreams like you."

"Huh. Oh yeah." I was just thinking about me teaching Jerry to play baseball and basketball. "He's a good kid and deserves a father."

"All right, make the appointment. Here's my phone number at Jackie's. Just let me know when." She wrote down her address, too.

"You l-live with Jackie?" I was picturing that conversation the first time I called there and Jackie answered the phone. Well, she forgave her sister. Maybe she would have forgiven me. But I'm not blood.

"Well, how else could I afford to raise a fatherless child?"

I was ready to tell her to get a job. "Don't try to make me feel guilty. You could have told me years ago. Alright, Jerry's coming back...shhh."

"Okay, I'll talk to you soon. Oh, can I have the other half of that bill?"

"As promised." I handed it to her then bent over to Jerry's side. "Nice to meet you, Jerry. Maybe we'll see you soon."

"Thank you for lunch, Uncle Jim."

Chapter 47

Babysitting:

"So, it looks like I might have a new nephew," Larry said. "A lost brother and a lost son all in one week. Sure you're not ready to get lost?"

"No, I'm not going anywhere," I said. "But I've got a lot of thinking to do and a phone call to make…actually a couple of them."

"That Josie still looked pretty fine. For an ugly sucker like you," Wayne said. "So, you moving back to Albuturkey sooner than expected?"

"I'm not sure. Just not sure." I had a lot of thinking to do but the first thing needed was the setting up of a paternity test. And, no pressure, but sometime before I leave in the next four days.

Having a cast iron stomach came in handy right now since the last couple of days were tougher to digest than a bottle of Tabasco.

"Don't be so down, Bubba. My job sucks and my life sucks. Except for my son. Little Wayne makes my life."

I imagined a kid like my friend Burt's son Corey. He was a good boy but he was still a boy whose curiosity got the best of him sometimes. When there was any activity, Corey got himself in gear to do it. Unfortunately, he also got the car in gear if you left the doors open or left him waiting in it. One time, we even had to get him out of the middle of the road.

But he was well adjusted although his parents had gotten divorced. I had no desire to get together with Josie even if Jerry was my son. She was still a con artist. If Jackie was telling me that she had a son with me, I probably wouldn't even ask for a blood test.

"I work with a guy whose wife works at one of those blood-testing places," Wayne said. 'Let me call him and try to see where it is."

"Thanks, man. Maybe things will work out as easily as Larry got a place to live."

Ronnie didn't have a phone set up yet so we took off to Wayne's to use the phone; myself, who used to go out with Ronnie when he was Veronica; Larry, who just ended a ten-year relationship with a transsexual, and Wayne, who'd had his lone metaphysical encounter at Morphy Lake. I wouldn't be surprised if Benjamin showed up.

But maybe Ronnie was keeping him away. Or maybe Wayne was. Either way I was glad he wasn't around. But maybe he could help me figure out if Jerry was really his great-great-grandson.

***

"Duty calls," Benjamin said to Victoria. "I'd better get dressed."

"You're going to leave me here all alone! After you got Larry to break up with me, you're going to leave me in this Indianapolis motel room."

"It won't take me long. They'll strip me of my title and, worse, cut off my penis if I don't respond."

"I don't know. Go, go. You've already ruined my life."

***

There were few times in my life when I really needed a beer but this was one of those times. I went to grab one out of the fridge.

"So, Jerry's a good kid," Benjamin said. Now I needed a six-pack but then I realized my driving and babysitting duties came first.

"What in the hell are you doing here?"

"Came to check out my new great-great-grandson despite my great-grandsons' lack of respect for me."

"You get the respect you earn...but you think he's my son?"

173

"Not for sure yet but it looks like it. I have to be drawn to him and I'm only feeling that a little bit now."

"I don't even know why I'm talking to you. You're probably just looking to find another trannie to get together with. So you can throw Victoria away after ruining her life."

"You don't understand!" Benjamin went on to explain how his duties involved only looking out for the Goodmans and making our lives better. "Vicky was, and I stress was, good for Larry but things had run their course and she was too old for him, anyway."

"But you're not too old for her?"

"My existence can't be counted in years. I made the deal a long time ago to serve my family and if I get a little nooky on the side, so be it."

"Sort of a guardian angel with a little Goodman or Epstein devil thrown in."

***

Wayne got off of the phone. "Let's go."

"Where? Don't forget. We have to put little Wayne back in the car seat again," I said.

"Where else? To get your blood drawn."

"I have to get a hold of Josie so she can go."

"Easy, killer. You don't have to go at the same time. We'll get yours drawn and call her to set an appointment."

"How much?" I was doing okay moneywise but my checkbook was still recovering from some of the medical bills from my cancer. The only scars that hadn't healed were the ones on my wallet.

"She thinks she can do it for free. There's a student who needs to do a paternity test to get her final certification. UNM Medical School will pay for it."

"Wow, how cool is that? I owe you a beer."

"More than one...12-pack."

"I'll get you a friggin' case." Who needed money when beer had become our wampum?

Wayne's son finally cried; he'd eaten and drank earlier so there was only one more reason for him to cry. After the diaper was changed, it

174

was time to put him back in his carseat. At least he was having a good time.

"At least if Jerry is my son, he's past diapers and carseats."

Chapter 48

Testing Our Blood and My Patience:

"Josie, I'm at a lab now and will be getting my blood drawn in a few minutes," I said over the phone. "What time can I bring you and Jerry over here tomorrow?"

Lobo Labs was across the street from the Pit, where UNM played basketball, and catty-corner from the school's football stadium. While it had the sterile smell of a medical office anywhere, its walls were adorned with numerous posters of past and current UNM athletes.

They should have a lot of experience with paternity tests—what with the Lobo football team's track record.

"Boy, you sure are in a hurry? Guess you're trying to make sure I don't change my mind."

"I have a non-refundable airline ticket to New Jersey tomorrow. And I have to go back to work on Thursday. Want me to lose my job?"

"You're going to leave your son and me to fend for ourselves?"

"You do understand that if I lose my job, I won't have any money?"

Josie changed her tune real quick. "What time do they open?"

The nurse told me they opened at eight but that was a little too early for Josie. We agreed on 9:30 AM

"Let me talk to Jerry real quick."

"Sure you want to talk to your son before the test? What if it comes out negative?"

I wanted to tell her that I would take Jerry with me since he'd be better off without her in his life. But I said, "He's a good kid either way...oh, what's his last name? Can't I talk to him to see if he wants pancakes or eggs for breakfast tomorrow?"

"Hewwo, this is Jewwy Gooman."

"Huh, oh...hi, Jerry. Do you like pancakes or eggs better for breakfast?"

"Both...and bacum."

"Okay, good. We'll get some tomorrow. Can I talk to Mommy?"

I wanted to tell her that I knew she had just told her son to use my last name when talking with me...control, control.

"All right, so I'll pick you guys up at 9:15 and we'll go out to eat after they take Jerry's blood."

"You don't have to take us out to eat afterwards." Her voice seemed different as well as her attitude.

Was she showing real compassion or just trying to set me up for something bigger? "It's okay, I already promised Jerry. If you have somewhere to be, we can just get something to go."

***

The needle jab hurt and the student phlebotomist was having a tough time finding my veins. It wasn't the first time that had happened in my life. More than a few people would say that you had to get past the ice water to find my blood.

But he finally hit and the vials were filled so I could leave. I should have stayed another minute but the ice water in my veins had melted.

***

I really hadn't thought about it as I was getting pulled over. I was thinking more about why the cop had his lights on behind me. I wasn't speeding, both headlights were working and I hadn't run a light, since there weren't any,or a stop sign.

"License and reg...," he drew his gun and asked me, in no uncertain terms, to step out of the car. Keeping my hands in plain sight, I complied. Then it hit me. The fake blood from my job. He's gonna' think I did something.

177

"Hands on the hood; have any weapons or anything sharp in your pockets?"

"No, sir. What's this all about?" He searched me and found nothing.

"Where are you coming from and where have you been in the last half-hour?"

"I'm coming from the Halloween Scary House down the road. I was working there all night...what's going on?"

"Can anyone back you up? You're in a vehicle that someone saw leave a violent crime scene and your clothes have a lot of blood on them ."

I tried not to laugh because it sounded like a serious situation. "It's fake blood I put on for my Halloween role and there are a lot of old red Chevy trucks like mine. Can you take me over there so we can straighten this out?"

He cuffed me and loaded me in the car's back seat. Everyone had gone home except for Frank, who ran the business and had just gone to sleep.

"He's worked here before but he wasn't here tonight," Frank said.

I was still in the car but could hear him. "What...check my timecard! There were a lot of people working. Maybe you're just still half-asleep," I yelled.

He retrieved the cards and looked through them. "Let me see. Goodman...no, no Goodmans worked tonight."

"This is crazy. Call Abby 555-1270. Joe 555-8200 and Paul 555-7950. They all worked with me tonight." Remembering people's phone numbers was something I knew would come in handy someday.

Frank offered the use of his phone.

"Yeah, hi Sarge. Dewey here. I have a James Goodman here who had the victim's phone number, is covered in blood and is driving a vehicle fitting the one the witness described. His alibi didn't check out and I'm bringing him right over."

They got all the blood that they could from me including that on the hospital gown I was wearing for my role as an escaped mental patient. I was given a pair of shorts to wear since the gown had been my only garment and I got some temporary booties instead of the shoes they took also.

"We'll have to test all this," Sergeant Pepper said to me. "If it's fake blood, that will come up."

I was locked up, for the first time in a long time, yet still able to sleep due to my full confidence in the legal system. I was awoken and brought into a room to do a lie-detector test just as the sun came up.

"Passed it with flying colors but some sociopaths can," I overheard the polygraph examiner tell the captain.

The captain went to talk to Pepper. And Sergeant Sargent Pepper, he had pointed out that was his first name like the Kennedy family's Sargent Shriver.

"I have some good news and some bad news. There was some real blood on your gown and body. But there was also some fake blood. And your friends Paul and John both said you were working last night at the scary house."

"So, I'm free to go," I said while collapsing from the realization that Abby had been killed.

Meanwhile, Frank was gassing up his red truck with Abby's stolen credit card. He called his girlfriend to make sure the cabin in Milagro was stocked with enough food and water for a while.

Chapter 49

Getting In Deeper:

"Bro, I don't know how to thank you enough for the hookup," I said to Wayne.

"I can think of at least 12 ways for you to thank me, maybe eighteen. But a case of Bud might be asking too much," he answered.

"Tell you what, I'll get you a case of Bud now and bring you an ice-cold pony keg of Genny Cream next time I drive out. If I can borrow your car today after I take you to work."

He laughed because he knew that it couldn't be done. "I'll be satisfied with a couple of cases. C'mon, I'm gonna' be late for work."

I dropped him off at the base golf course where he worked. Tijeras Arroyo was as close to Manzano Base on Kirtland Air Force Base as you could get. I had played a couple of rounds there, the only real golf I ever played, since they were closed on Mondays and we got to use the carts with nobody else on the course.

But all I could think about were the missile silos hidden in the mountains. A leftover from the now-ending Cold War. A good portion of America's defense and offense came from a radius of just a few miles from here since Sandia Labs technology had been on the cutting edge since WW II.

But what about golfballs that went straight. There had to be technology for that. Anyway, the mountains were beautiful on this morning as they usually were and Wayne was off to trim the greens.

I took off to Jack's since I had a little time to kill and he didn't know about my latest news. I didn't know what his reaction would be. On one hand he'd want me to return sooner and on the other, he'd always told me not to have kids (or get married) if I could help it.

***

"You look like shit. Aren't things working out with your brother? You know it ain't gonna' be easy after all that time," Jack said.

"No, things are working out great with him; he's already got a place to live. Just never thought I'd be unhappy to be coming back here sooner," I said.

Jack had a lot of business acquaintances but not that many friends. He looked happy to hear that I might be moving back in less than the two years I had planned.

"You won't have so much of a smile when I tell you the reason why. Pretty sure I have a son. I took the blood test today."

"I told you to be careful—shit, your life is gonna' change."

"I'm not a hundred percent sure yet but it sure seems like it. Remember that girl I brought over here once. I told you she has a twin. Well the twin, I was only with her once, has a son that would be the right age."

"Hopefully the poor kid doesn't look like you."

"Huh. Oh yeah, he looks like me, acts like me, eats like me and even daydreams like me. I take him for his blood test in a little while."

"That beer money will soon disappear...it will start going for food and sneakers and clothes and medicine."

That's the irony of it all. You have more worries and less money for the beer you need to forget about them. But Jerry seemed like a good kid despite his mother. If I had a son, there was some solace in the fact that he was a good one.

"Damn, I just want to get this over with so I know if he is my son or not. I can deal with the outcome of the test. I just can't deal with the waiting."

Jack had never taken a vacation since he was pretty motivated business-wise. He and his sister Maria had purchased a cabin at Sumner Lake a couple of years ago, about three hours away, where he had spent a few weekends. I thought he was stressed out but I would have taken a weekend at his lake house over the weeklong vacation I was having.

"I feel like just going to hide at the lake for a couple of days until I know what's going on," I said.

"Here's the keys. Take your brother along if you want."

***

"Now these I can drink," Jack said as we sat around the fire watching the last minutes of the sunset at the lake. I had been trying for years to get Jack to have a drink with me but beer was never his thing. Now I found that he could be tempted with wine coolers.

If there was one thing I was good at, it was corrupting people. I had gotten both Meri and Margie drunk on their eighteenth birthdays. But my skills weren't limited to younger people since Jack was ten years older. He's a big guy, close to 300 pounds, and it's funny to see him slurring his words after just two coolers.

Actually, he gave a couple of sips of the second one to Boomer.

"Guess I'm stuck with the rest," I said. "Unless I cook some burgers on this fire. Maybe after dinner you can handle another one."

Jack went up to get the burgers out while I placed the grill over the coals. He tripped but caught himself going into the cabin, which was built into the side of a hill.

"There's more steps ahead, you lush, better let me get the food before you go through the glass door!"

Jack sat down and admitted that I was probably right.

"God might take care of drunks, but I watch over those I make foolish by getting them drunk. Maybe better than I watch over myself."

Jack laughed while I got the burgers, buns, plates and fixins from inside. About fifteen minutes later, I was climbing the tower to ring the ship's bell perched atop it.

Boomer yelled to me, "Where are you going? Careful of that…"

"Shit," I yelled as the step broke underneath me. Luckily, I hadn't stepped right in the middle of it or I would have dropped the ax I was going to use to ring the bell. "Rest of the steps okay?"

"Should be, just be careful!!"

I was bound and determined to ring the bell for dinner. The top of the tower gave an incredible view of the lake with the full moon rising. I thought to myself that persuading Jack to do a little night swimming might not be that hard to do in his current state.

But, I rethought that, after we spotted a boat nightfishing right where we usually swim next to the ramp. After dinner, I went for a solo dip after Jack and his son passed out.

***

"I'd better not take those keys, Jack. I might never leave there."

Chapter 50

Are You Laying Down, Dad:

With Jerry and the added complication of worrying what I would say to Jackie if she answered the door, it was lucky I made it to the apartments accident and ticket-free. I sat in the car just inside the gate for a minute to gather myself.

"Checking up on your son," Benjamin said.

"It's no wonder a lot of people don't want to be alone. They must have guardian angels who sneak up on them too."

"So you may not believe me but I'm not feeling it."

"Very funny. A double negative from a negative son of a bitch saying that Jerry is my son."

"No respect for everything I've done for you."

"Yeah, what's your angle this time? I'm gonna be late. Go back to Victoria so you can leave her ruined like you did Larry."

"No respect. Just mark my words!"

"If only these gates were guarded by St. Peter, you would never have been able to get in here!"

Although the complex did have a gate, they were far from luxury apartments. They were in a shaded neighborhood which there was a dearth of in Albuquerque. For areas to have tall trees, they had to both be old and not have had the trees chopped down to make room for more homes or utility lines.

The way Albuquerque was growing, most of the lots which were empty just five years ago were filled in with homes and businesses. Since the city could not expand north, south or west due to Indian reservations or east due to the mountains, subdivision of lots was the last alternative for builders.

The Las Lomas neighborhood had always been one of my favorites when I lived near the university. It had some big "old money" homes right next to UNM but just a block away, there were affordable homes and apartments. It was close to public transportation and both freeways if you had a car.

"You coming inside anytime soon? Oh, you were hoping just Jerry would come out." Identifying her face was difficult against the sun but it was definitely Jackie's voice.

"Yeah, I was trying to avoid a confrontation with you. Too much going on to deal with that. Still mad?"

"I forgot about all of it a long time ago. Holding grudges only makes life more difficult."

"Guess I could learn something from you. It's good to see you. Well, it will be once the sun is out of my eyes. Apparently, I've been blinded for seven years."

"Well, I'm glad you don't think I'll castrate you. Because we may be tied for at least another dozen or so years."

"You mean because you're Jerry's aunt?" She looked sort of like she was nervous about talking to me. Staring up in the air for the words.

She finally found them. "You haven't really gotten the full story yet. Josie isn't really Jerry's mom. He calls her Mommy because he's with her a lot but he calls me Momma."

"Oh, Momma. Could this really be the end? What are you saying. You're really Jerry's mother?"

"Yeah, and you were the only one I was with during the time period of conception. Josie takes care of Jerry during the day while I'm at work."

185

I was still getting Bob Dylan out of my head. I was ready to revisit highway 61 or any highway. "But, but…but she's using him to try to grub money from people."

"Yeah, Josie's got her own problems but she would lay her life down to protect Jerry from any harm."

"And I guess you didn't tell me because of our breakup? You didn't forgive me for a couple of years, then."

"Jerry was only a couple of months old when I tried to find you but you had stopped shooting darts as much by then. I thought if it was meant to be, then it would happen and the weeks became months then years."

My life was similar to Larry's in that I felt like staying close to someone was an unattainable goal. Every time it started to happen, I felt crowded and pushed them away or they just left. Yeah, Larry had been with Vicky for a while but I think he felt like he owed her for saving his life.

"I don't know what to say. Are you with somebody now?" I reached out for her hand and caressed it softly. Just hoping to comfort her.

She accepted it and I could feel her veins pulsing. "No, I'm not but we have a long way to go for a house with a white picket fence."

"No cats in the yard , life is still pretty hard. But everything would be easier because of you."

"Come on, we'd better go. We'll be late. I'll get Jerry."

"Don't need the blood test anymore. Totally believe you."

"We should still get it. In the back of your mind, you would always be wondering." She was making sense. I couldn't deny it.

"Alright, let's go."

Josie came running out of the apartment "Your brother's on the phone; he wants you to come get him."

Every place in Albuquerque was within fifteen minutes if you lived near the freeways. I ran over to get the phone and see what time it was.

"I can't miss Jerry's appointment. They're doing me a favor, Larry. If you get over to Central and take the bus down, I'll come get you." I gave him instructions including which stop to get off. Going straight down Central was an easy trip which would only take him about fifteen minutes and fifty cents.

"Hi, Jerry. How are you doing today?"

"Good, but hungwy."

"We'll go eat in a little while." I put my hand on his shoulder and we walked out the door and down to the car.

***

The lab finished with Jerry Chavez, not Goodman, and we picked up Larry on the way back to Jackie's. He was a little bored but I also think he wanted to hang out with me since he didn't know anyone else who wasn't working.

"Wow, he does look a lot like you…but better looking," Josie said, looking at Larry.

"Yeah, he's a little taller and I'm a little wider. It depends on if you want something to grab onto or not. Hey Jackie, can I use your phone to call long distance... I'll pay you?"

"Sure, Jim. It's alright. Take the cordless outside if you want."

I dialed my father's number but didn't want to stay on the phone long. "Hi Dad. You have a grandson."

"Yeah, I know. Andrew and another on the way from Don and Sue."

"Well, yeah but you have one in New Mexico now, too."

Silence "Dad, you there? You there?"

"Jim, this is Susan. Your father passed out. What's going on?"

Chapter 51

Moving Back to New Mexico:

So, my life was going south or southwest to be exact. I was moving back to New Mexico again. Bonus, my dad was coming to see Larry and Jerry. Certainly not the trip I was expecting at the time I was expecting to do it.

"Hey Don, guess Thanksgiving is out this year. Looks like I'll be in New Mexico." I had called Wayne's brother Don, who now lived in Virginia. I'd spent a lot of time with Don and his family whether they were going to Long Island to their hometown and I met them there or Norfolk.

"What the heck. Thought you weren't going back for another two years?"

"It's been a heck of a week. Actually it feels like a month but it's only been four days. Remember my youngest brother that's been gone. Well, we found each other. In Albuquerque."

"That's great. Doesn't he want to go back East again?"

"Not just yet. He likes it here and is just readjusting to normal life. But there's something else."

"What are you wanted for in New York this time? Besides the cribbage debts you owe me."

"Very funny. Not even a traffic ticket there...well, none I haven't paid anyways. You know how I've always lived life free and easy. Even more than you because I have no responsibilities. Well, that's changed."

"What the hell?"

"Remember those twins, Jackie and Josie, from when we used to shoot darts? Well, I kinda' hit a bullseye and...."

"And you're getting married? After just four days?"

"No, at least not now. But it turns out Jackie had a son and the poor schmuck looks like me. Acts like me, even farts like me."

"Holy crap! He's your kid!"

"Well, we're getting the blood work done now but it's just a formality. Everything seems to point to the fact that the seven-year-old boy is mine."

"Kathy, Kathy!!" Don was yelling to his wife. "Jim's a father."

"Wait, which Jim are you talking to now? I thought you were talking to Jim Goodman."

"I am, I am. He's pretty sure but they're comparing the blood as we speak."

"I'm almost as surprised as you guys are. But I'm starting to make plans. You driving cross-country anytime soon?"

"No, but the Ford truck needs to. I've been planning on giving it to Wayne." Don was a true oldest brother who took his role very seriously. Taking care of his five siblings, even his friends, whenever needed. He'd become the man of the house at a young age when his parents got divorced.

"Cool, we'll get it up to New York at some point and I can pack it with some of my stuff." I could leave just the essentials then pack the van in New York when I was ready to go permanently. Friends like Don helped things to fall into place.

"Yeah, we can work things out when you come back to New York."

"Cool, I'm on someone else's phone anyway." This was just one of the many things I would have to be working out such as work, breaking my lease and a few other minor details.

***

189

Larry and Josie had struck up quite a conversation while I had been on the phone. Both of them had spent a little time living by their wits. In just a few minutes, Larry had revealed more to her about the past decade than he had to me.

I was trying not to pay too much attention as I was figuring my future out with Jerry and Jackie. I hoped Larry wouldn't follow in Josie's footsteps since it seemed like he was getting his own life more on track than he'd had it in the past ten years.

We had our separate conversations going on. Both of them intense in their own ways. I saw the two of them holding hands at different points in their conversation. But they weren't talking about how to raise their son. I can guarantee that.

Pretty soon, Larry and Josie went off to be alone.

"We're gonna lay down and watch TV in the bedroom," Josie said to Jackie.

"Okay. We'll be right here," her sister answered. "Jerry, you don't need anything out of the bedroom, do you?"

"No, Momma."

I was glad Larry had met someone to hang out with yet just a little leery of Josie's motives. But I couldn't be my brother's keeper.

"Just leave the door open, kids," I said.

Larry knew I was joking. "Yeah, right," he said as he closed that door. Little did he know he'd also be opening a new one.

Chapter 52

Making Plans:

"So, Don…guess I'll be doing a lot of moving in the next few weeks. Helping you finish your move to Vermont. Then me starting to move to New Mexico," I said to my brother Don.

He hadn't heard yet about Jerry. "I thought you weren't going back for a while."

"Yeah, well something came up. About seven years ago. Andrew has a cousin and you have a nephew."

"What? Wait. Yours or Larry's?"

"Guess."

"Just tell me, you son of a bitch."

"If I'm a son of a bitch then so are you, technically. Mine; hit the bullseye with a girl I met while shooting darts in 1982."

"Wow, all I can say is wow! You have had a busy week."

"Guess getting busy in '82 wasn't the best move…or maybe it was. So I'll be moving back to Albuquerque over the next few months."

"You're positive, right?"

"Well, I'm still waiting on the paternity test results but the poor little guy is a carbon copy of me from his love of basketball to his hatred of combs touching his hair."

"I'll be back tomorrow and we'll talk more. I'm on someone else's phone." I loved that line since I hated talking on the phone.

Jackie and I were continuing to figure things out as Larry and Josie emerged from the bedroom.

"Anything good on TV? I think "M*A*S*H" is usually on in the afternoon," I said to them.

Their smiles belied the fact that nothing had been watched with the TV only on to muffle the sound.

"We should get going, Jim. I've got some stuff to do at the new place."

"Like fixing it up a little and finding a job," I said.

He gave Josie a kiss while I gave Jackie and Jerry a hug as we departed. "I'll stop by tomorrow, I said."

"Me too."

On the trip to Wayne's, Larry told me that Josie had a line on some work for him. Something that could prove very fruitful. All I could do was hope that it wasn't something illegal.

***

"You got an extra parking space? You're gonna' be gettin' a truck in the near future," I said to Wayne.

"What, did you become a seer this week?"

I told him about Don's truck and he stayed right in character; pretending not to be happy. But, down deep, we both knew that he was a truck guy. Not a Hyundai guy.

"So, you're gonna' start moving back in the maroon truck?"

"Yeah, it's all but official. Jerry is my kid."

"Poor little guy. Where's your brother?"

"Dropped him back off at his place. He's got a line on some work through Josie, he said."

"I wonder what that might be...you think it's legal?"

"One can only hope."

***

My plane was taking off at 1:30 PM so I went to Jackie's around 10:00 am to say my goodbyes, at least for a couple of weeks. Larry answered the door.

"Discussing work prospects, little brother?"

192

"Among other things. This bus system does work pretty well, huh."

"Yeah, maybe a little too well. I brought breakfast but I didn't know you'd be here."

Jerry was watching cartoons and I helped him eat while Jackie was getting her second cup of coffee. I had a piece of green chile on my chin. The same spot where Jerry had a piece of bacon glued with maple syrup.

"Dang, you boys look right at home," Jackie said to us.

"Yeah, and so do your sister and my brother." The pair was sitting there talking non-stop until there was a honk outside and they exited, getting into a new Beamer with an Oriental man in an Italian suit.

"I'll be back in about an hour," Larry said.

I told him that I would be here for about ninety minutes before leaving for the airport. I never trusted men in suits and the situation seemed strange but Larry wasn't thirteen anymore.

"I don't ask any questions until I have to post bond. Only had to do that once," Jackie said. I found out that Josie had been convicted for soliciting but I was assured she had changed her ways.

Chapter 53

Making the First Move:

I don't know how John even knew Don and Burt but somehow they all met me at the airport with a box of "It's a Boy" cigars. People were congratulating me in the airport and asking how much he weighed. Funny how they stopped smiling when I told them he was 36 inches and 41 pounds.

"Your poor wife," one stranger said.

"Oh, we're not married. But he is seven years old now. I just found out about him."

I got a lot of cigars back by telling people that.

"Congratulations, Jimbo," Johnny said.

"Thanks, man, thanks. How did you meet Don and Burt?"

"From a New Mexico picture after one of your camping trips. We just met at the airport. I came to pick you up."

"Oh yeah. And you two assholes just drove up from Virginia?" Burt lived just south of D.C. at the time.

"Why not?" I knew it was Don's idea. Burt probably had to change his schedule around to do it but Don never had a schedule.

"Boy, these are some lousy cigars. Better wash 'em down with a snifter of brandy." Everyone concurred and we found a little airport bar.

"So, Don, guess you're gonna go out to the Island. Burt, I know how much you love New York."

***

Burt had to have a slice of New York pizza on the way to our canoe trip in the Adirondacks.

"They probably won't try to greet you in any way. But if they do it's time to go to another pizza place. Congeniality and pizza just don't get along. I think it's the 900-degree ovens that these macho pizza makers have no control over," I said.

Burt grew up in the South and thought I might be pulling his leg. He walked up to the counter, "Howdy!"

"Huh," the attendant wasn't used to people greeting him.

"How you doing?"

"Busy." There was an awkward New York pause. "What can I get for you?"

We ordered and it was pretty good. But Burt made a decision.

"I'm never coming back to New York again. The pizza was great but I just can't stomach the people here."

***

Don and Burt went to Atlantic City on their way south while Johnny gave me a ride in the opposite direction.

"So, with all the hubbub about Jerry, I didn't even tell you that I found my brother Larry."

"Quite a week in New Mexico, Jimbo. Double congratulations."

I told him that Larry had decided to stay there. John already knew that I was going to be moving back out West.

"Let me know if you need some help packing and stuff." Almost anyone else and they would have been jokingly saying that to speed me up but John was just being supportive. He was one of those few people I would miss.

"My last name will be Mayflower for the next few weeks. First I have to help my other brother move to Vermont."

Don wanted to do some work on the truck before we brought it up from Virginia. So that gave me enough time for two trips to Vermont in-between working both jobs.

***

195

"It's kind of weird, huh? My new son might have hand-me-downs for the son you've had for three years," I said to my brother as we took a break after loading his moving van.

"Life is weird. I could have still been in New Mexico except for Liz. The Goodman boys will probably never be together in the same place."

"After finding Larry, I think almost anything is possible. Mark my words. One day we will get together, our kids included."

A faint cry could be heard. "Right on cue. Boy, that sure sounded like it came from the direction of the truck."

"It can't be…" Don went running into the house, then came running back out a few seconds later. "Andy's not where I left him."

We both ran over to the truck, calling his name. "Where could he have hidden? There's no furniture or anything else big enough to hide in," I said as we heard a slightly louder yet muffled cry from the back of the truck.

"Kids can hide anywhere. You'll see."

We were frantically unpacking and moving things around until I heard Don say loudly, "I'm going to punch this soft guitar case just to see what it does."

Andrew unzipped the case and popped out saying "Ta-da!"

"His favorite guitar was in that case; he probably didn't want it to go without him."

We loaded the second truck and were soon on our way to Vermont. About a four and a half hour drive. Andy was in his car seat, asleep for about four of those hours, with his favorite guitar in its case next to him.

Chapter 54

Gathering No Moss:

Vermont was kind of crunchy in October. The leaves had long since changed and most had fallen. Drying out while waiting for the first snows to fall. I could have seen myself living there, in the summertime.

But at least it was comfortable to unload the truck into Don's home in Poultney, not too far from Rutland. We'd both slept well the night before and were done unloading by 9 AM. I got a quick tour of the old Cape Cod-style home, the quaint New England town and the breakfast menu at the local café.

And we were headed back to New York to return one of the trucks and reload the other after Andrew had shown us how to rake the yard. He'd made a pile of leaves as tall as him but at least he didn't hide behind it.

As we got back on the Northway, I thought about my year at Paul Smiths College. It was just a couple of exits north to access it.

***

Poof. It didn't hurt until we realized we weren't getting out of that snowbank without a tow truck. It was already late Sunday night and, much as I liked to party, I didn't want to miss any classes on Monday either.

It probably wasn't the best weekend to go home in February. But George, Eric, Mike, Bill, Gary and I were undaunted by the predicted blizzard. It had been a fun weekend at home and we were drinking in George's station wagon on the back road from Keene Valley when the snow caught up to us.

We took care of the important things first. Getting the beer into the snow so it wouldn't freeze at eight degrees. Then we took turns by the side of the road trying to flag someone down. Every time we changed off, another six pack entered the vehicle. There wasn't a lot of traffic but we knew people up here took care of each other.

After about a half-hour, the second car stopped. The woman asked us if we wanted to warm up before she drove five miles to the nearest pay phone.

"No, that's okay. Unless you want to take one of us with you," I said.

"Yeah, we kind of want to get out of here," George echoed my sentiments.

"My boyfriend has a truck with a winch, he'll get you right out. C'mon. Come with me." She was pointing to me.

She asked me if I was warmed up just before we got to the gas station with the phone.

"Mostly." She kissed me while she put her hand down my pants. "How about now?"

"Much better."

"I'll be right back after I use the phone." She came back in a minute to finish warming me up.

"H-how far away is your boyfriend?"

"Ten minutes; he's not really my boyfriend. He just has a crush on me."

"So he gets jealous…"

"Yeah, that's the fun part."

I pulled out, he pulled up and we were pulled away from the snowbank another ten minutes later.

***

Driving was the perfect opportunity to daydream as long as you didn't wander all over the road. Once I was in driving mode, the truck

198

could almost go on auto-pilot without me even realizing how far it had gone.

It helped to look at the dash every once in a while. Especially the gas gauge. When I was doing long trips, the gas gauge became real important since I wouldn't drink anything until I got to a quarter of a tank so there were no inbetween bathroom breaks.

That didn't work with a three-year-old in tow. But we still made it to New Paltz, about an hour from home, in about four hours.

***

It was beautiful weather when we left on our April camping trip to the Shawangunks, just above New Paltz, New York. Lee, Steve, Kim, her cousin and I set up camp by the lower falls; parking my Charger about a hundred feet across the creek from our campsite.

It was a peaceful, fun night until the snow began to fall about 8:00 PM and fell quickly it did. There was about a foot within a couple of hours and we decided to go down to the college dorms in town, about twelve miles down a windy road, We left our tents up and took off before things got even worse with the roads but there was a lot of partying going on at the teachers' college and we high-schoolers were having a hard time fitting in With all the bodily fluids and prone bodies in the hallway, we thought better of that idea even after a couple of Jack and cokes with a couple of tokes

So we slept in the car and drove back up to our winter wonderland to climb around in the falls for a few hours before we left.

The weekend ended on an up note until the speeding ticket I got on the way home. I wonder if Steve still has any of those pictures climbing around below the falls.

***

And we were home in time to load up Don's Vermont-bound truck, go to work and then take the bus to Atlantic City to meet my friend Don with the other truck to take out West. At least I'd catch a nap on the bus and make a roll of quarters for taking it. More than enough for the tolls on the way home.

199

Tolls were just one more thing I wouldn't miss about the East Coast.

Chapter 55

Family Pictures:

Since everybody was headed in different directions, Dad (really Susan) wanted to get a family portrait. Now, I didn't mind getting my picture taken as long as it was a natural shot. Never liked getting dressed up and trying to get my curly locks to stay in place.

"I just wish Larry was here for this. Could be the last time all the Goodman boys are in the same place," my father said.

"We talked about this, Dad," I said. "You know Larry is just easing his way back into becoming an adult." I showed him the Polaroid recently snapped of my youngest brother

"I know, I know. There's just got to be a way; he looks so old and I've already missed his last ten years."

"The only way is to get everyone down to New Mexico 'cause Larry's not leaving anytime soon."

The phone rang and it was Larry. He was asking my father for his address so he could send a letter that would explain a lot of things.

"333 El Dorado Drive. Spring Valley, New York 10977," my father said. "Yeah, I'm trying to get down to Albuquerque but haven't worked it out yet."

***

Indeed, Josie had figured out a way for Larry to make some money. Illegally. This wasn't even in a grey area. It was definitely not legal to marry someone for money to help them get their citizenship. The Oriental man with the Beamer, he went by Johnny, had a friend who was wanting to move to the United States permanently.

Jian Chang was already here on a student visa which would be expiring in a month. She would pay Larry a total of $15,000 to marry her for five years, at the end of which would be a citizenship swearing-in ceremony.

So Josie would get $1,000 just for setting it up and Johnny would get some undisclosed amount while Larry would get $3,000 just for going through with the initial stage. He would get the remainder in monthly increments for the duration. The civil ceremony was already set up for the next day after Jian flew in that afternoon.

There were a few Chinese attendees plus Josie and Jerry, who was the ring bearer. Everything about it looked like a real wedding day except for the exchange of money afterwards.

***

"He was still in the City two weeks ago; he's been there most of the last five years," Duane told his friend.

"You got the gun? Getting the money back from that kid was all I could think about the last few years. I owe you for picking me up," Berry said. "Man, it feels fuckin' good to be in civilian clothes. Let's get out of here."

"I still can't believe that mother fucker hid those diversion hoses and cordless drill in my place. The cops came just in time to find them with my prints on them. I deserved to go but that fucker should have gone with me."

"You never know who you can trust. He's changed his name then changed it back. I think that he's let his guard down in the last five years."

Larry and Berry had met when my brother was sleeping in buses. Berry had worked for Greyhound and knew more than a few seedy characters hanging around downtown Pittsburgh. Larry only knew the bottom ones on the street but Berry knew a few that were higher up on the totem pole.

One night on a deserted platform in the bus station, a mysterious man made them an even more mysterious offer. He would pay them $10,000 and get them out of some previous trouble to let some water out of a coolant tank.

"There's got to be more to it than that. What is the tank cooling?" Berry was doing the talking but Larry was just as curious.

The man had a suitcase. "Here are the tools and $5,000."

Larry went to grab it. "Gloves!! Leave no traces!" The guy was straight out of film noir; he opened a brand new pair of rubber gloves with his gloved hands. "Your instructions are inside, too. Do not open this until I am gone but we will meet down in the boiler room tomorrow at the same time. You can either return everything or tell me that you accept."

The cloak and dagger guy turned around and started walking away when Berry opened the case. In one fell swoop, the delivery guy was back with one hand on Berry's throat and the other squeezing his testicles.

"Follow instructions," he yelled. "You'll be doing your government a huge service." He turned back around satisfied that he had gotten his point across.

And he had. They weren't sure about taking the offer until Duane misappropriated $1,000 out of the bag –Larry and Berry had no way to return the money. Three days later, the meltdown at Three Mile Island due to a water leak was known worldwide.

Two months later, Larry was in witness protection after turning on Berry. The U.S. Marshals hid him for five years.

Chapter 56

Surprise:

The appointment was made with the photographer for two days later, and Don and I showed up reluctantly. I hadn't combed my hair or worn a tie as requested but I had long since stopped doing either one.

The inside of Susan's house had nothing masculine about it so we decided to do the Goodman boys portrait outside. We would come back in and the ladies would join the picture.

I brushed my hair and begrudgingly put on a borrowed tie before going outside.

"Can't you tighten that tie?" my father had told me the same thing since I was six years old.

"Yeah, Dad. Where's the scotch? I may need some soon," I said facetiously.

Don was all ready to go and wanted to get back home so he could finish packing. Andrew was better behaved than I was but that could change quickly.

Meanwhile, there was a knock on the front door. "Does Allan Goodman live here? I'm his son," he said to Tessie, a little hard of hearing.

"I didn't catch you. Can you speak slower?"

Larry spoke slower and louder. The volume only made things worse.

"Hold on," Tessie said. She called for Susan, who recognized Larry right away as she rounded the corner.

Susan surprised herself by being able to put the words together.

"Hi, I'm Susan. Wow, it's great to meet you! Really great...let's go around the back. You're right on time even though nobody expected you. Your father is going to be ecstatic."

"Hold on, hold on. I have somebody else for the picture," Susan said as she walked around the house.

My father was ecstatic to see Larry as evidenced by the mark he left on the grass when he passed out. Even Don was a little excited. But I wondered how Larry had gotten the money to get to New York so quickly.

"You're not going to make him put on a tie for the portrait? He's still the baby of the family," I joked after getting Dad revived.

The photographer, as they always seem to be about something, was angry about having to shuffle people around since Larry was the tallest instead of me. But we got the keepsake done.

I didn't want to ruin the reunion by asking any questions but Larry could see how I felt. Especially since he'd been hanging around Josie. It was the best day for our family in a long, long time.

Don's wife Sue left early and started packing while Don watched Andy and bonded with the brother he hadn't seen in ten years. Dad tried but he was an emotional wreck

Larry had been through so much in the past decade that nothing fazed him anymore. "I have to leave in two days," Larry said.

"Y-you can't stay a little longer?" Dad replied.

"I have responsibilities in Albuquerque. I can see why Jim likes it so much out there."

"Where are you staying while you're here? C-can you stay here?"

"Sure, if there's space. I want to catch up but two days should give us plenty of time."

Dad spent those couple of days fawning over Larry like he was a kid again. Much like he had tried to do with me when I had first come back from out West.

"I'm gonna go out with my friends from the restaurant tonight. No need to wait up," I said to Dad. Staying in the finished basement at Susan's house for the first month I was back in New York, it was necessary to tell him, in my mind.

"You don't ever drink and drive, do you?"

"With the traffic and the way people drive around here, I can't drive without drinking first."

He didn't broach the subject again.

I didn't spend much time with Larry in New York since I'd soon see him again in Albuquerque. My father could have all the time with Larry that he wanted and so could Don. But the three brothers did go out for a beer one night.

"Did you guys ever have a beer together? Because I know I never had one with Larry," I said. "Cheers." We clanked our bottles.

"Yeah, I bought Larry a six-pack once and we did some LSD together. Ended up going out for some more beer since we drank it so fast," Don said.

"Yup, I remember laughing my ass off that night," Larry said.

"You both know I never did any psychedelics til I lived in New Mexico," I said. "Sorta made a deal with Mom and Dad that I wouldn't do anything stronger than cannabis while I was living with them. I did try coke once in college but I didn't like it anyway. The batch we got was too speedy."

Don had brought his guitar along to the smoky, old jazz club we had gone to. Be-Bop Tango. He knew the guys in the quartet who were playing. They asked him to sit in for a little while and said, "Now sitting in with us is an accomplished guitarist soon heading to Vermont, Don Goodman."

"I haven't been introduced publicly since I played high school football," Larry said after Don was welcomed onto the stage.

205

"Yeah, I meant to ask you about that. The last I knew you were kind of a nerd who collected coins and read World War II books. What happened?"

"Well, I grew for one and I found out girls liked guys who collected yardage better than guys who collected coins. I was able to run pretty quick due to kids chasing me all the time."

"So you returned your first kickoff for a touchdown and did pretty well even after that. What made you leave the first time?"

"Life was kind of a downer outside of school with the folks divorced. I would go to Dad's every weekend to hear shit about Mom and vice versa during the week."

"Yeah, I don't wanna make this night a downer but I just thought I'd ask. Don sure found his groove playing the guitar, huh."

"That he did, that he did."

Don came back from his set and I held the salt shaker up as a microphone. "Don Goodman, you just played a brilliant set. Would you say your older brother was your biggest inspiration?"

"He was; he inspired me to keep my door locked so he couldn't come in and mess up my practice time," Don said.

Chapter 57

Finding Larry:

Vicky recognized the guy at her door but she wasn't a hundred per cent sure where she knew him from.

"I was looking for Larry Goodman. I'm an old friend from school," Berry said. Duane was hiding around the corner so as not to intimidate Victoria. Or just in case Larry went out the rear window of the old brownstone.

"He doesn't live here anymore. Last I saw of him he was headed for California," she had realized Berry previously worked at the Greyhound station and remembered that he had gone to prison.

"Alright, just tell him Dave was looking for him. He'll remember me."

"Will do, Dave."

Berry went around the corner to see Duane. "She's lying through her teeth. I think she recognized me."

"We'll wait for her to go outside after dark and see if we can't get the truth out of her," Duane said. "In the meantime, let's get some fruit off this vendor."

"Yeah, I haven't had some good, fresh fruit in a long time. Eat a peach?"

***

"Hey Jim, whatever happened with our dog? You took him with you to New Mexico," Larry said at dinner the next night.

I didn't want to tell him the truth. "He lived until he was seventeen. Took him to the mountains more than a few times."

* * *

It was the strangest-looking animal I'd ever seen. Sasquatches, if they were real, didn't live in the Pecos Wilderness in northern New Mexico. Not that we'd ever heard of, anyway. But it seemed to walk erect, sort of like a cross between bear, gorilla and human.

Peppy, my pet retriever mix since I was eight, was barking like crazy at what he didn't know either. He and I were on the same wavelength after growing up together while taking many camping trips. We had almost named him Hippie. What can I say, it was the sixties, man.

Richard was fumbling to keep his camera straight, Juan was looking for his .22 rifle and I was just looking.

Who knew how, but the women were still sleeping through all the commotion. Or so we thought.

"What the hell's going on out there?" I wasn't sure who it was; Kimberly, Carla or Stacy.

I calmly went to the door of the tent, explained that there was a large animal nearby and that quiet would probably be a good idea. "It's only an elk but he's a bull and in rutting season, we should try to stay out of his way. It's his time of the year but I hope it's nobody here's time of the month."

"Mine's coming up but not yet, thank God," Kimberly said.

"We're good," all three girls were awake now as I could hear the other two in unison.

"I'd advise you all to stay in the tent until he moves away; he doesn't seem too interested in us right now."

Carla didn't like being taken care of. "I've got my pistol, I'll come out." She came out wearing only her .38 and a pair of 36C's. There was definitely something about the seventies that I was going to miss when they ended in a couple of years.

208

She hadn't turned around and seen the beast yet. It hurt me to say it but my next piece of advice was for her to get some clothes on. I figured that would buy us a few minutes.

Carla tossed me her gun. "Here, just in case!" I was glad my soft hands were able to catch it although using it was another story with my lack of experience. "Oh, and here's the bullets."

Meanwhile, the creature had turned toward us from about a hundred feet away and made several quick warning charges our way. We weren't too startled but Peppy thought it was his job to protect us by charging back. Richard cursed as he couldn't get the animal to stand still.

"Nobody's gonna believe this shit without a picture. Not to mention a shot would be worth a few bucks to some magazine," Richard yelled.

Juan yelled back, "If he takes another step this way, he's gonna get a different kind of shot; he might not like that one quite as much."

I walked over to get a beer out of the river where we had left a six-pack in a calm area to stay cold. Our visitor had messed up my campout custom of a sunrise beer. I don't know if it was just the shine of the cans or what but he came charging towards me when I got the six-pack out of the ice-cold water in Jack's Creek.

I threw one towards him before dropping the rest back in the river but Peppy was already on him before he could reach the can. In the most amazing combination of grace and strength I'd seen in a wild animal he grabbed the eighty-five-pound dog in mid-air and cradled him, gently placing him on the ground. He would live peacefully another two years until he hopped a six-foot fence on the Fourth of July 1979 at age fourteen when I'd been convinced to leave him behind on another camping trip.

I felt a strange calm come over me as the creature got his beer, tapped it a couple of times and pulled the ring back.

And that was how I'd met Benjamin. Although he didn't tell me who he was.

***

"You know, Jim, I think maybe I'll stay a few more days here. It's kinda cool to have everyone together without you and Don hitting me in the back to stop me from talking," Larry said.

"Or without dad turning around and yelling at us for doing it," Don said.

I didn't want to go there but I did anyway. "So where'd you get the money to get here?"

"It was an advance on a job that Josie got me."

"What, has she got you running drugs or smuggling people across the border?"

"Nothing like that."

"Making porn or selling your body?"

"Jim, leave him alone! Larry's not stupid."

"Yeah, I guess now is not the place or the time."

***

Berry and Duane were patiently waiting and Vicky exited her house about 8 pm. Duane put his hand over her mouth as she passed the alley and Berry jammed the gun into her left side.

"I'm gonna ask you again if you know where Larry is. This time you'd best give me the right answer, Victoria the bus driver."

Duane released just enough to let her answer. "I told you. He went to California."

"You do know who I am, right. I'm Berry who Larry put away in prison for ten years. Tell me!" He jammed the gun into her ribs enough to cause intense pain.

"We were together in New Mexico until last week. He got pissed at me and he's still in Albuquerque as far as I know."

"You're full of shit, bitch." Berry slapped her.

She was crying. "Look in my purse, the receipts are in there."

Duane looked and held them up when he found them.

"How do we know he was there? You could have gone with someone else," Berry said.

Benjamin, coughing a little more often, showed up and took care of the evil-doers with a lead pipe. Not out of any kind of chivalry; he just wanted another piece of ass from Vicky. And he could help out Larry at the same time.

Chapter 58

Still Looking:

Larry and Dad were going over some old pictures when I came to Susan's the next day. My father was overjoyed that Larry was staying a little while longer but I realized that it would make things that much tougher when he did leave.

"Hey, mind if I join. I haven't seen this album in a while," I said. I'm usually bored by such things but this was kind of a unique occasion.

"Life was free and easy back then," Larry said while looking at a summer vacation picture from Acadia National Park in Maine.

There was a lot of laughing and reminiscing for an hour or so. Until we came to the one picture.

"I remember thinking that I was the greatest photographer for catching this at age thirteen or fourteen." Larry was running and I caught him in mid-stride without blurring it.

The sad thing was that when he'd disappeared, I always thought of that picture. It was clear Larry was running but was he running away from or towards me? Especially after Mom had called me in New Mexico," I put my arm on my brother's shoulder.

Our family didn't show a lot of affection. That was the first time I remembered Larry and I hugging.

***

"Who in the hell was that guy with the lead pipe? He came out of nowhere," Berry said to Duane with both nursing their wounds.

"I dunno. But I think Vicki was telling the truth this time."

"I can't leave the state, never mind the country. How am I gonna get to Mexico? I'll never get a damn passport," Berry said. The ex-con was talking to Duane in his accomplice's Bowery apartment.

"It's New Mexico, not Mexico. You don't need no damn passport. That's right, you were out smoking pot during geography class." Duane had to talk loud over the shrieks of a cat versus rat fight in the hallway. A pistol going off ended that fight.

"Hopefully, they only killed the rat. How do you live here?"

"The rent's cheap."

"My fuckin' rent was a lot less in jail and it was cleaner than this. There's more lead falling from the ceiling than that guy had in the pipe he used to chase us off."

The pair were planning their trip to Albuquerque when the dim lights went totally out.

***

"Another blackout. At least I don't need the heater or the a/c," Vicki said. "I hate this place."

"I don't know. You seem pretty hot to me right now," Benjamin said.

"Funny, very funny," Vicki said across the king size canopy bed. "I wish things would have worked out so Larry and I could've stayed out West. It's all your fault."

"Ah well, Larry's back in New York for a few days. I could be coerced into telling you where."

"It's all your fault, all your fault." She was pounding him on the chest and he was hacking like a lifetime non-filter smoker.

"That's no way to treat me .I'm the only one who can make you really feel better."

"I hate you, I hate this, I hate everything about you. Get out, get your hands off of me."

213

Benjamin knew all of Victoria's turnons but none of them were working. His plan had backfired like his lungs were, this time.

"If that nefarious pair comes after you again, I'm not gonna be there to help you."

"I don't care, I deserve whatever I get from them."

Benjamin slammed the door, tripped down the steps and floated a little less softly to the sidewalk than he had in the past.

***

Victoria began meticulously looking through the phone books at the library for Allan Goodman. She knew it was a longshot but finding Larry before he left again was the only way to keep her small amount of sanity.

My family was uncommon but my last name certainly wasn't. At least two L's in Allan narrowed it down a little but there were still a lot of them in the suburbs.

She started writing down names and numbers but quickly got writer's cramp. Vicky decided to make copies of the pages with the A's and Allans on them, unless there were only one or two.

In that case, she would still write them down to save her dimes for copies. It would be far too expensive to use the pay phone in the library since all the calls were out of area.

Chapter 59

Research Pays Off, Sort Of

She was almost home with the Nassau, Suffolk, Bergen and Rockland county pages when Duane and Berry approached her. Duane's knife made a hole in the A. Goodman's as he lunged in an attempt to scare their victim.

"Asshole, you made an A-hole," Berry said.

"I'm trying to find Larry's father; hopefully you didn't cut up the page with his number on it," Victoria said. It felt good for her to not be afraid of the pair. "Dumb shit."

"What'd you call me, bitch?" He was reaching for his gun.

"Wait! We still need her help. Me thinks Larry is not in New Mexico for the moment," Berry said. "Or why would she be looking for the little runaway's father?"

The pair escorted Vicky home and decided they would "help" her.

"I'll look in the Bergen and Rockland pages while you guys check out the Nassau and Suffolk," Victoria said.

"But Larry was in Bergen County when he was in high school," Berry protested.

"He always thought his father would go back to the Island where life was a lot happier," she replied, knowing that his father would most likely not do that.

Vicky's plan worked. It took about an hour for the pair to give up on calling numbers, mainly with no answer. And a couple of times when they got through, they'd dialed the same number twice.

"Paperwork was never really my thing," Berry said. "We'll be outside. Don't try to leave without us."

"Yeah, yeah, yeah. Blah, blah, blah." She knew the bus stopped at 4; 52 AM And they would never be awake then.

Now to try some numbers. No answer at the first five Allans. Then she remembered there were copies of the business pages she had made too.

Larry's father had his own business. Marketing. She tried the Bergen business section first but soon moved to the Rockland book where Allan Goodman Associates in Spring Valley seemed to jump off of the page.

Vicky made the call and my father answered the phone. Her hard work had paid off; patience, patience until the wee hours and then, catching the bus.

***

Berry and Duane lurked outside, keeping each other awake until it hit about 2:00 AM "I think we need to take turns staying up," Berry said. "Otherwise, we're just gonna talk each other to sleep."

"Standing guard standing up. That's like being in the damned military," Duane replied. "But it's probably the only way we'll stay awake."

"Let's draw matches to see who goes first." He tore them out of the pack he always carried with him, then took a piece of trash to hide the ragged edges. "Short one takes first shift."

Berry got the short end of the matchstick. "Guess I'll get to sleep in two hours."

Duane was already snoring.

***

At 4:30 AM, Benjamin was hot-wiring the '65 Lincoln. "Ah, I haven't lost my touch," he said as he bypassed the ignition wires, got a spark and heard it start.

He had a feeling that Vicky was going to try and catch the 4; 52 bus and he was going to be ready to give her a ride. And maybe take care of the scoundrels chasing her at the same time.

He drove a couple of blocks and was parked a few doors down from Vicky since alternate-side parking had cleared that side for the street sweeper. He was idling and saw the bus round the corner at 4:51 AM but had his eyes on the street sweeper creeping up behind him at 4:52.

Vicky quietly exited her house and was running across to the bus in sneakers while Benjamin was still looking in his rearview. He turned around to see her scamper onto the opposite side of the street.

Meanwhile, the combined decibels of the bus and the sweeper caused both Duane and Berry to stir. Duane saw Vicky running across the street and took off after her with Berry not far behind.

Benjamin called Vicky and she recognized his voice. "Get in, Vicky. Get in!" He was pulling up to let her in the driver's side rear door.

But, with the switch not working on that side, the door was still locked after Benjamin thought he had unlocked it. He turned to unlock it, not realizing that put him on a direct course for Duane and Berry.

Chapter 60

Collision Course:

Larry awoke just before 5 AM, rocked out of his dreamworld with a crash. He went up out of the basement apartment to the kitchen, made a cup of coffee and sat down in the den to watch TV.

With all the excitement of the last few weeks, between reuniting with people and uniting with new ones, he hadn't had much time alone. Even his not-so-fairy godfather had shown up while he was in the bathroom.

Larry was half-awake when I came walking through the front door and, hearing the *M*A*S*H* repeat, entered the den.

"You felt it too, huh?" I asked Larry. His eyes were open but his brain was closed. I sat on the opposite end of the couch awaiting his awakening as my eyes slowly closed.

I was soon jolted by a scream from Larry yelling, "I shouldn't have done it, I shouldn't have done it!"

"Done what?" I was awake but he wasn't. I woke him just in case he was about to have a panic attack or something.

The repetition of my question finally brought Larry to say, "A lot of things starting when I left home."

"You did something stupid again recently, huh?"

"Can you keep this in the strictest confidence? I could get in a lot of trouble, again."

"I don't want to see you leave when you just came back. How bad could it be?"

"Well, I married somebody for money. Yeah, it was through Josie."

"Damn. I knew that girl and you hanging out was bad news. Well, I'm no angel, either."

"Really, what did you do?"

"I was moving a lot of pot in high school and before I went to New Mexico. Even grew a little in the backyard in Hillsdale."

"Oh, that was years ago. That ain't nothing."

"It wasn't that long ago when I grew it in Albuquerque and sold it off of my roach coach. I sold some hash, too... while I was slinging hash making seven hundred burritos a day."

"That doesn't even compare to what I did. Doesn't even come close."

"What the hell did you do? Kill someone?"

"That's a story for another day. I want to make sure you don't let this one out first."

"If you can't trust your brother, who can you trust?"

"I'm not even sure that I can trust myself."

***

He tried his hardest to limp away from the accident before the first responders showed up but Benjamin could not muster up the strength. Whatever immortal powers my fairy godfather had left had been sucked away during the collision.

In an attempt to avoid hitting Berry and Duane, the car thief had killed Vicky with the rear door. For a few years, Lincoln had made those back doors open backwards and she was hit by the "suicide" door at a speed fast enough to throw her under the left rear tire.

As Berry and Duane made their escape, with Vicky's flying memo pad in tow and a few wounds from jumping out of the car's way, Benjamin was lamenting over Vicky's loss. Sorrow was something he

219

hadn't felt for over fifty years and it was compounded with the guilt of killing the woman he had been taking advantage of.

The door glass had shattered and it didn't take him long to find the right size piece.

***

"Looks like this one lives right here," Officer Krupke pointed across the street.

"Yeah, I think she was running to catch my bus," the driver said.

"I can't find any ID on this one. At least nothing more recent than 1938," Officer Squire responded. "He's old but I don't think he's a hundred and twelve."

It was quite a scene to come upon for the normal person who was leaving for work. What with a bloody man on one side of the car and the tow truck lifting the rear of the Lincoln to expose Vicky's lifeless body.

But not for the New York City detective who arrived as her corpse was being removed.

"This is typical of the city at night," Detective Sherlock NoShit said. "It's a vehicular homicide by suicide door combined with a vehicular suicide by suicide door glass. Just another night in the city."

"Should have been driving a Chevy. Damned Fords will get you every time," Krupke added.

Chapter 61

An Unlikely Hero:

"What are you gonna do this weekend besides the birthday party? It's weird coming home from college, huh," I said to Meri.

Picking her up at college in Albany for her grandmother's birthday, we had decided to come back on the east side of the Hudson taking the scenic Taconic instead of the boring Thruway. It was a little slower but also sans tolls.

"Yeah, it's weird. Especially having the rules which I'm sure I'll have once again," Meri said. "And I'll miss my friends at school."

"Yeah, it'll be tough to have a Meistie whenever the urge hits you, huh?"

"You make it sound like I drink all the time. I'm not that bad."

"No, not all the time; here, have a real beer." I handed her a Heineken after opening it with my teeth.

***

Duane and Berry needed to come up with a couple of bucks after their cuts had healed some and their black and blue had turned to red. "Let's just knock some old fart over the head," Duane said.

"No way, we got to stay below the radar a little. I get caught doing some shit like that and I'm back in the federal lockup."

"What do you recommend, then? Working day labor like some minimum wage asshole?"

"Alice still have that restaurant down in the Village? At least we could get some meals out of a day's work there and the work ain't that hard."

"Shit, if I liked washing dishes or peeling potatoes I'd still be in the Army."

"C'mon, man, it's just for a day. Let's lay low until we catch up with Larry. That was a close call with that old Lincoln."

"What are you, scared all the sudden?"

"I just don't have a good feeling. Just do this for one fuckin' day."

"Alright, you owe me big time."

"Like the Beatles said. Yeah, yeah, yeah. I told you I would take care of you."

***

Meri had met up with some friends and they'd decided to go to Manhattan. She was more of an Upper East Side girl but her friends had talked her into checking out some galleries in SoHo, then heading to the Village for some night life.

As college kids, it was a fun glimpse into their futures to look at the artwork that could someday be hanging on their walls or sitting on their end tables. But that could really work up an appetite. Especially when a night of partying was ahead of them.

"Look at this place. You can get anything you want; at least that's what the sign says," Dara said.

"Except for Alice. A pretty strange name," Meri replied. "But we are in the Village."

Josh had been looking at the menu. "The menu basically gives a list of twenty items and says you can get any combination or single item. It's pretty crowded; let's check it out."

"We don't all ride a motorcycle. I just like standard fare," Dara said.

"Look, you can just get your burger if that's what you want. And it doesn't look too expensive," Josh retorted.

Meri was scanning the place. "There's a lot of weirdos in here; some of them must be locals. It's gotta' be good if Village people come here."

"Yeah, as long as The Village People aren't playing," Dara said, smiling at Josh. "We already have one macho man."

Josh looked around like he didn't know who Dara was talking about and the trio went to be seated. The menu was a little confusing so they just ordered sandwiches; Dara got her burger, Josh got chicken and Meri an Ahi tuna on Focaccia.

The waitress brought out a basket of kosher dills just like in the old days.

"I don't want a pickle, just wanna' ride my motorsickle," said Josh, reading one of the many signs on the wall. They had been born a little too late to get the Arlo Guthrie or sixties theme.

"Hot Tuna Burgers," Meri was reading another sign. "I guess that's what I got."

The food was both plentiful and good. The group left sated and moving a little slower than when they had come in. Perhaps that explained what happened a moment later.

***

"See, it wasn't that bad, was it? A little food and a few bucks," Berry said to Duane as they were leaving the restaurant.

"I guess…but we could have made a lot more a lot quicker boostin' a car."

Berry saw another benefit of an honest day's work. "Besides, I can tell my P.O. that I'm working here. Even part-time will keep me from doing time."

"We gonna' go find some women. I know you must want to after ten years…look at those two over there with that dude."

"Don't point; I'm on a mission first to find that money. Then I'll worry about women." They began walking towards the group of teens near the curb just as a crosstown bus approached.

The brunette took a step and her medium-length heel broke, sending her plummeting over the curb and directly in the path of the bus. Duane

223

jumped and was able to lift her out of the way save for her right thumb, dislocated by the front bumper.

"Oh, thank you so much," she said looking at the man who seemed a little down on his luck. She was still a little shaken but offered him a small token of her gratitude which he totally took the wrong way.

"I live just a couple of blocks away; Just walk with me," Duane said.

Meri corrected him. "No, I meant a few dollars."

"Just take it and don't start any shit," Berry said.

"I can't take any money from you, ma'am."

"Well, are you hungry or anything?"

"No, we just ate. Just remember this if you're ever on a jury at my trial."

"Alright…well…thank you."

When Duane turned to leave, he glanced at Meri's license he had nabbed and something about it struck him. But he tried to put it away so nobody would notice that he had it; he was unsuccessful as Josh had seen the money wrapped around the license just like Meri had pulled it out in the restaurant.

He spotted what looked like an unmarked police car across the street, pointed at them and yelled "Cops." He then took a dive at Duane's arm as he'd been tucking the fake I.D. away. Josh's instincts were right as Duane and Berry were both a little frantic about the cops.

The license went flying one way and the nefarious pair the other way. Josh handed Meri her money and license while she was picking up another piece of paper that had floated to the ground.

"Thanks, Joshie. You're my knight in shining armor."

Dara was visibly shaken. "I'm not sure about going out tonight but let's get out of here before they come back."

"What the hell? This piece of paper has my address on it," Meri said as she unfolded the note. She hailed a cab going the opposite direction.

Chapter 62

Larry Prepares to Go Home:

Dad wasn't doing real well since Larry would be leaving that day, Don would be moving soon and I would be taking my first load out West in a few more weeks. He and Don weren't ever really on the same wavelength but things had gotten better as the middle brother had grown into adulthood.

And even better when he'd given him his first grandchild, or at least the first one that he knew about. But, in Larry's case, Dad didn't know when he would see him again.

I was planning on taking Larry to fly out from Newark in the afternoon so the Goodman men, not all good men, were having a brunch. For brunch, alcohol was more socially fashionable so we had earlier decided against breakfast or lunch.

I had yet to tell anyone about the call I'd gotten from Albuquerque.

***

"I'm looking for Mr. James Goodman. This is Jodi from Lobo Labs."

Luckily, it was me who answered the phone at Susan's house. "Yes, this is he."

"I have your paternity test results and usually recommend prospective fathers sit down."

"I already know the answer. The kid's all mine. I don't need to sit."

"Sometimes it's difficult when reality really sets in; have a seat."

I lied and said I was sitting. It was a good thing that I was right above a chair.

"Jerry Chavez is not your son; definitely not."

"Huh…what? Somebody made a mistake. The samples got switched or something."

"There's no mistake, sir."

"Alright, thank you. I can get a second…" Dial tone.

***

"Are you sure you have to leave? You could just stay a couple of more days," Dad said to Larry.

"I told you; I've got a new apartment, new job…a whole new life and I want to do this on my own," his youngest son answered.

I warned my father not to press Larry like he had always pressed me to press my pants. That advice had fallen on deaf ears.

"It'll all come together," Don said. "Namaste."

The Eggs Benedict and Mimosa combo made for sparkling conversation as I think we all realized the Goodman boys would never again be in the same place at the same time. And we just came to enjoy it at the Stony Point winery. The venue offered a beautiful view of the Hudson from the Palisades. It was one of those parts of New York state that outsiders would never believe was less than an hour from the Big City, where deer and smaller wildlife roamed freely during the day. Bear Mountain, only a few miles north ,was aptly named and the big omnivores were plentiful but smart enough to be out mainly at night.

"The Goodman boys will be in all corners of the country but our hearts will be together," I let a little sparkle out from the rear as the sentence ended.

"I think you meant farts, not hearts," Don said just before the brunch became reminiscent of the campfire scene in *Blazing Saddles*.

We shooed the waitress away between guffaws but could do no more after our neighbors began leaving and she called the manager.

"You are just having way too much fun," the woman manager said to all of us in general. She looked at my father but quickly gave up on him having any authority when he burped and we all laughed again. "You guys ready for the winery tour?"

"*Mas vino de pata*, sure," I said.

"We don't crush the grapes with our feet any more. Too much toe cheese. Not as good with the wine as baked brie," she said. "I'm Cassandra, they call me Mama Cass."

She certainly didn't have Cass Elliot's shape. "I guess you can sing," Don said, always looking for new musical talent.

"Listen, I can toot the first stanza of the national anthem," Dad said. He proceeded to attempt it but lost it on the fifth or sixth fart.

"Show us to the wine cellar. We're all getting fat except Mama Cass," Larry said.

She was smart enough to walk us through the grounds before we went to the tasting room. Cass pointed to a pile of old vines, "That's where we throw the grapes for the deer after we crush them. After a while they ferment and the deer can be seen dancing the night away."

We all chuckled until I ran over and scooped up a handful. "Don't do it," Don yelled

"When did you become the sensible one?" I inquired while tasting one grape. "Blech...the deer can have them."

We walked the grounds and Dad passed out on the bench just outside the cellar where we learned how to make sparkling wine in the Methode Champenoise style.

"So we rotate the bottles...," Cass was interrupted by me asking for a catcher's mitt to go with the mask and chest protector used to save workers from exploding corks.

She was undaunted as she went on to explain spinning the prone bottles one-eighth of a turn every two weeks for about three months.

"I'm thirsty," Larry said.

With no more of the tour left, Mama Cass took us to the last stop. We were instructed to work from the dry whites to the sweet reds and then the sparkling wines. Luckily, I had taken Dad's keys earlier and, through a unanimous vote, we decided to let him sleep.

227

When Don returned to pick him up a few hours later, my brother was regaled with the story of our father awakening to a couple of drunken young male deer attempting to be dominant over him from the posterior.

Chapter 63

Acting on my Gut:

"I still know he's my son but something happened with the bloodwork," I told my brother Don the day after Larry flew back. "Don't say anything to Dad."

"Wow, you must really be sure."

"I'm telling you—if you saw Jerry for just two minutes, you'd know he was mine."

"I guess someday we will see each other and he'll meet his cousins. So what's the plan?"

I told him that I was just moving things up a little in order to take another blood test in New Mexico. This time I would pay for it.

"And you know, I don't really need any help with packing the last load. Sue and I will just be taking our cars."

"You'll let me know if you can't find Andy."

"His favorite case is already in Vermont; hopefully he hasn't picked out a new one to hide in."

Don would take off to Vermont in the next week. I would leave a few days later provided that I could get the truck from Virginia soon.

That was the next phone call on the list and Don Trimarchi always made things easy. He was coming to Long Island that weekend and said he was just about to call me since he had gotten the truck checked out and oil-changed.

I would meet him before he left Jersey and went into Staten Island at one of those rest stops where you could envision Jimmy Hoffa being killed and/or buried. But only if Hoffa was eating fast food, getting gas or, more likely at his age, in the men's room.

Don, although he didn't often do it, would call his brother Wayne. He'd let him know that I was bringing the truck in the next couple of weeks and I would let Wayne know when it was on its way in order to give him a couple of days heads up.

***

"So, I'm sure it's just a mix-up but the lab called and said I was not Jerry's fath....," I was interrupted by Jackie.

"But, but we both know you're the father. You're not chickening out, right?"

We'd been talking almost daily since I'd been gone and she knew how I felt. But I couldn't blame her for saying that after seven years.

"No, no, no. It just means I'm coming out earlier so we can go for a second test. Things must have just gotten mixed up."

"Guess you get what you pay for. This time we'll pay for it."

"I like the sound of that."

"Huh? Paying for it?"

"No, us as we. After all this time, the greatest mistake in my life is being corrected."

"Love you."

"Like the sound of that even more. Love you and Jerry, too."

But Josie I wasn't so sure of.

***

As I began packing the summer clothes not needed until next May, I was flip-flopping on whether or not to save one pair of flip flops. They were especially good for driving and you never knew when there would be that unusual warm day, even in the late fall or early winter.

I never had a lot of clothes so, after two boxes of summer stuff, I was onto the memorabilia which I would never need. The Yankees were pretty far from even a wild card and the Jets were in the usual bottom of their division.

Even though it was early in the season, I held out no hope for the Jets going anywhere except for the same place they had been since Joe Namath had left. And my Yankee cap was who I was even though any new possible Mr. October had been hibernating since August.

So the yearbook, old pictures and the turquoise squash blossom all went into the next box with the sports stuff. So if I heard about one of my old classmates doing anything from saving a sea lion to killing their spouse, I wouldn't be able to look them up for the next couple of months.

A few pieces of furniture and some pots, pans and knives would finish things off until I actually got the truck. Then I could see what would fit.

Just one thing I hadn't thought about; where was this stuff going to stay until I settled into a new place in Albuquerque?

I called Jack to tell him about my plan and he offered for me to leave my stuff for a few months in an empty rental. It wouldn't cost me anything but the house was about eighty miles west of Albuquerque in Milan, old uranium mining country.

Chapter 64

Purple People Eater:

We'd had some good times in Don's truck but some weird things had happened, too. One of his friends had borrowed it once and said he heard the bottom drag on something but found nothing there. He may have been lying because Don had to get the suspension fixed.

Then there was the crazy trip to the Gila Wilderness, the craziest of many I'd made there.

***

It probably hadn't been a good idea to go with our one friend Wylie, who had a coke problem, but things didn't bode well from the start. I'd been friends with Don for ten years, even stayed at Don's house for extended periods and had seen him and his wife quarrel a little.

But, while we were packing the truck, they had the worst fight I had ever witnessed between them. I told Don that maybe going out camping wasn't a good idea and should have stuck with that after our long delay in leaving; however, I let him talk me into the trip during which we got lost going on a "shortcut" which sent us on an eight-hour jaunt in the dark through the northern side of the Gila National Forest and its dirt roads.

We ran out of gas about a mile from the paved road and about another twenty-five from the nearest gas station. Don took off hitchhiking with the gas can, leaving the two of us to push the camper in the same direction. With a little help here and there, we made it about five miles before we saw Don passing the other way in a truck. We waved frantically and hoped he saw us.

He did and, now a day behind, we took off the way we knew to get to the Gila. But once camp was set up, Wylie decided it would be fun to find different ways to attack our tents all night. We tried to find his coke stash so we could hide it from him but were unsuccessful.

We went home a day early. But I later heard that Wylie had traded his cocaine problem for a gambling addiction.

***

Don and Kathy had left Virginia in separate vehicles about 6:00 PM and they avoided the D.C. traffic by staying off of I-95 and mainly on 301. It was a slower route but more predictable timewise so I could probably hope to meet up with them around midnight in Jersey.

I got there a little early since John, who was giving me a ride, had to work early the next morning. I grabbed two slices at Sbarro's then, exiting the food court, I was surprised to see Don's truck pulling in and shocked to find two rather scroungy looking guys getting out.

"Oh, I thought you were my friend from Virginia. Sorry," I said after seeing their New York plates, hoping I hadn't freaked them out too much.

"That's okay…hey, you got a couple of bucks gas money? We're kind of stuck here if not," the passenger said.

"I'm a little short right now but here's two bucks. I been there before."

"Seriously, you've only got two bucks? You're probably driving a brand fuckin' new car," the driver said.

"I'm drivin' a ten-year old car for what that matters. Get the hell away from me and be happy for what you got."

"Leave him alone, Duane. Under the radar, remember," his partner said.

I was walking away when Don pulled up in the truck with Kathy right behind him in their Toyota. They were visibly nervous and even their kids were awake in the back seat.

"Sorry if we're late, Don got pulled over but not for speeding like usual. Apparently, there's a truck like ours that got stolen a few miles from here," Kathy said.

"Stolen? Did y'all pass by any cops in the rest area. I think I know where that truck is...don't look but it's right behind me."

"Yeah, there was a cop right by the northbound entrance," Don said.

I got in with him and we drove over to the state cop positioned there. He took off like a bat out of hell to the truck I directed him to and the truck took back off the opposite way, fast enough to blow a piece of paper off of the dashboard. They entered the turnpike the wrong way and quickly got into a head-on crash with a peach truck. The stolen vehicle went up in flames immediately. Before either Duane or Berry could escape.

I went back over to where they'd been parked and found the paper left behind in the chase. "What the hell? This piece of paper has my dad's address on it."

"It's never just a normal day with Jim Goodman," Don joked.

"This just seems like a normal day for me, lately." I got Don's keys, entered the purple people eater and all three of us took off northbound in separate vehicles.

Chapter 65

The Battle before the Battle of the Bay:

"You're not going to believe this, Jim" Larry was telling me on the phone.

"I would believe anything this month. If you told me a planet full of vampires was going to hit the earth and flood it with the blood they'd sucked, I would be making final preparations."

"Yeah, okay."

"So you're not going to tell me?"

"My wife Jian has an uncle in Frisco and he's flying us up there next week. Do you know what's happening there next week?"

"Besides seventeen new gay bars opening and maybe a Harvey Milk memorial, I'm not sure what else."

I was a pretty big sports fan but with all the recent changes in my life, I hadn't thought in that direction. Larry had to clue me in that the World Series would be going on and his "wife's" uncle had gotten them tickets to a game.

"Shit, that's cool. At age twenty-six, you will have gone to a Super Bowl and a World Series. Just be careful with these people."

"You'd better be careful, too…'cause I have two extra tickets if you want them."

"What, huh…I can't go. It just wouldn't be responsible with all the things I have to do." I couldn't believe I was saying that; I had told Larry that the truck was mostly packed since I'd had everything in boxes before even picking it up.

"If you get here, he'll get you plane tickets too. He's got two restaurants and a few dollars."

"Yeah, probably not legal either. But I do need to get my blood tested again. I would just have to quit my job a little earlier than expected."

"And you could still work with Dad 'til you moved permanently. You would just need to get here by Monday, 'cause the game's on Tuesday."

"I could leave Saturday morning and be there Sunday night. Get an early start Monday and get the truck unloaded, then get my blood tested and fly out. You think he could be conned into getting me a ticket back to Newark instead of Albuquerque."

"Might not be that hard. Let me work on that."

***

How could I turn that down? It would be the opportunity of a lifetime to go to a World Series game no matter if I was indifferent to the Giants and A's playing each other; but then there was Jerry… oh yeah, and Jackie. As Tevye said in *Fiddler on the Roof* until there was no other hand, on the other hand he could break tradition and let the *nebuch* marry his daughter or, in my case, I could take Jerry with me.

But, on the other hand, where would I get the money for that? I needed to be start being responsible for my son's sake. And for my future with Jackie, I should be trying to put some money away.

If the Yankees were playing, it would be no question. But the Athletics and the Giants left me thinking about it. "Oh, come on, that's crazy," said Jackie on one side while her twin was telling me to go.

Josie was even pushing me to bring her along but that was my last option. I finally settled on being responsible. Taking Jerry wouldn't make up for seven years of absence but it would be a good way to get to know my son a little better. But if Jackie didn't want me to do that, I wouldn't because I truly wanted to give our relationship a chance this time.

***

"I think it's a good idea but how are you set financially?" Jackie was being sensible when she laid it out for me on the phone. "I think it would be worth pulling him out of school for a couple of days. Maybe he could do a report on the trip."

"Financially, I wouldn't do it except for the opportunity it offers. When will Jerry and I get a chance like this again? Besides, most of the trip will be paid for…the guy even owns a restaurant where we can eat most of our meals."

"And Larry would be okay with it?"

"I think so; he didn't specify that this trip was for adults only. Besides, he'll be spending most of his time with his new wife."

"Yeah, well…I won't say anything to Jerry until you talk to Larry."

I did and things must have been meant to be because they came together quickly. The plane, hotel and rental car reservations were made; Jerry was almost as excited about his first flight as he was about the baseball game. Not to say that he wasn't studying the team rosters every chance he got since he was telling me about each team's players when I talked to him.

My father wasn't happy about going from three sons around to none within a week but he had gone to a Brooklyn Dodger-Yankee World Series game once and he understood. Nonetheless, still unapprised of my blood test results, he couldn't wait to meet his new, yet eldest grandson.

Chapter 66

Reading Between the Lines:

I hadn't done a straight through solo trip across the country before then in any vehicle but I had driven from Montgomery, Alabama to New York in twenty hours and had made more than a few eight-hour trips to Virginia. My initial trip cross-country took me three months and my second took me about six weeks. But I was pleasantly surprised by how easy it was to drive 2,000 miles in Don's truck without stopping, except for gas.

I had already planned not to eat during the trip and to only drink when the truck started getting thirsty for gasoline. I also planned on leaving just before sunrise to avoid driving through two nights since 3 AM wasn't my most alert time.

Only one major mistake, though: I did start off a few M.P.H. over the speed limit but quickly found that was more tiring due to being on a constant vigil for state police. And everyone you talked to said the state police in their state were the worst in the country.

Once I got the speed adjusted, I got into driving mode or a driving trance reminiscent of the Jan Michael Vincent movie, *White Line Fever*.

The crowded roads of the Northeast Corridor quickly opened up once I hit Interstate 81 in West Virginia and only slowed a little once that road made the curve to I-40 in Tennessee and hit that state's cities.

There were but a few small to medium cities before Albuquerque and I missed all of them at rush hour. Even Oklahoma City, which one local had told me was so big area-wise that you would have to leave right after lunch to make it out of before supper.

October was also past tornado season so I wouldn't have to worry about dodging them.

I had been alone for over a day and thought about a lot of things from Jerry and Jackie to the redwoods near San Francisco. But then I wondered why Benjamin hadn't shown up even when I was in a gas station bathroom. Ah, better not think about him; he might show up and cause trouble.

Usually, when you have thirty-four hours alone, there's enough time to think your problems out. Or make them more complicated. I chose the former on some but the latter on most. Sometimes acting spontaneously is just the way to go and maybe that's the key to life, when to think before you act or when to act before you think.

But driving was not a microcosm of life. It was about living between the lines. It was okay to be inside as long as you weren't on them. But I had found life much better when you lived outside the lines.

I made it back to Albuquerque in less than a day and a half without killing myself or anybody else that I know of. My dad used to say that he never got into an accident but all three of us boys knew how many he'd caused; I could only hope I wasn't the same.

When I got to Wayne's house, I was hungry and tired or tired and hungry. Guess I was too worn out to set any priorities. It was 6:30 in the evening and Wayne said there was room in the shed for my stuff.

As ready as he was to act on that right then and there, I begged out by saying a little R and R was necessary. After standing up for a few minutes, though, we at least got the truck halfway unloaded and it was time to get myself unloaded. Or so I thought.

"Ready for a Bud?" Wayne said as he handed me a cold one.

"Are you ready for a Genny Cream? Somewhere in there is a cold one. It shouldn't take too much searching."

239

Wayne told me six hours later that he had found the Genny inside of three minutes. I didn't get to enjoy one with him since I had passed out after three seconds or one sip of my Bud.

I dreamed about Jackie and Jerry when Genny didn't monopolize my dreams. She was the only one I could get on tap.

Chapter 67

On Our Way to the Battle of the Bay:

Jackie had gotten the new blood test scheduled early so Wayne and I were up at the crack of dawn emptying the truck. After a quick going over, it was decided that I could use the camper that day since it hadn't even used a quart of oil or a drop of antifreeze.

I drove over to Jack's house just to give him enough time to call me an asshole for spending the money on baseball. I couldn't go to Albuquerque without stopping in on him and Linda with the kids.

As luck would have it, the front wheels started making a little noise when I was about a block from his house. The truck pulled up in front and the brakes were locked up as tight as the house at 7 AM.

A light was on in the kitchen where Linda was making burritos and breakfast for the kids.

I rapped lightly on the window, totally catching her by surprise since there was no forewarning of my appearance. She was happy to see me as usual and I quickly woke up Jack to let him know about my predicament. He let me use his car just to go to Jackie's and get the blood test after I explained what was most likely a mix-up.

"I'll get Boomer to check it out later; when he gets out of school," Jack said. At thirteen, Jack's son was already a pretty good mechanic who had his own car.

I thanked him, handed him Wayne's number and took the battery charger off of the station wagon that I would be using for the next couple of hours. The car's charge was about as positive as mine about the next couple of hours, or days in fact.

***

"Why don't just you and Jerry go to the lab this morning? It will give you a chance to get to know each other a little better…oh, wait. I'll have to sign off on them drawing his blood," Jackie said to me not long after we'd hugged upon my arrival. "But I'll leave you and Jerry alone as much as possible before you fly out this afternoon."

"That makes sense, yeah. It's gonna be a great trip; we'll be stopping in Vegas on the way to Frisco. Flying into Vegas is a cool thing even during the day with all the casinos and the rest of the trip will be the stuff dreams are made of."

"Yeah, I just hope he doesn't miss me too much. He's never been away from me and Josie for more than a few minutes." Jerry walked into the room. "Lookin' good, little man!"

He let one rip. "Ah, that's my boy. Nothing like an early morning posterior release to get the day going right. Me and him will be fine." I put my hand on his shoulder.

"I know he's ready to go. We got everything packed up last night. He's even been practicing using his chopsticks 'cause he knows he'll be eating lots of Chinese food. And he packed his glove incase there's a foul ball."

"Foul, yeah…I know one thing that's foul," I whiffed my hand in front of my scrunched-up nose. "Jerry's butt."

My son laughed and I thought he was ready for the match trick. I knew it was time when Jackie walked out of the room for a minute. "Okay, don't tell your mom I showed you this and definitely don't do this yourself. You take a match; light it and bring it around like so." I put it behind my butt and let one rip, thereby making a mini-flamethrower.

242

Jerry lost it; laughing, farting and peeing in his pants simultaneously just as Jackie walked back in. We all knew neither one of us really needed another blood test.

"That reminds me. Better pack some extra underwear," Jackie said. "But try to keep the farting in public down to a minimum, boys."

We got the test done and Jackie followed me to Jack's house to drop off the car with two hours to kill before going to the airport. "You don't have cable, do you? We can get some food to go and watch the World Series preview on ESPN."

"Yeah, you boys can watch while I make some green chile stew. You haven't tasted my cooking yet."

"That'll work."

Jerry and I hung out on the couch as the aroma of Jackie's cooking wafted its way through the apartment. There wasn't too much in the world that smelled better than green chile cooking. During harvest time, you couldn't drive through Albuquerque's South Valley without craving some while locals were roasting the fresh vegetable to peel and freeze for the winter.

"So, you've been learning about the World Series players the last few days; who's your favorite player? Mark McGwire…Will Clark?"

"I wike Candy Maldo…Maldonado; he's weally good and he used to play fo the Dukes."

"That's right. Yeah, I used to watch him play when the Albuquerque Dukes were really good. So, you're rooting for the Giants?"

"I'm not sure but I want Candy to do good."

What seven-year-old wouldn't want candy? "You know Candy is short for C…"

"Candido, yeah, the Candiman is the best."

Chapter 68

Jerry's First Flight:

"Larry, have you seen Benjamin? I think it's kind of strange that I haven't." I asked my brother after he introduced me to Jian in Jackie's car.

"No, and I don't miss him one bit," he responded. "Are you excited, Jerry?"

"Yeaw, I can't wait for Candy…"

"Here, I have some including gum which you should chew on the plane," Jian offered some in her hand.

Jerry corrected her on who his favorite player was but still took the candy.

"My son all the way," I said. "I think he's almost as excited about flying as he is about the game."

We drew closer to the airport and getting to know Jian made me like Larry's situation a little more. She captivated me with a couple of Frisco stories and those of her ancestors building the railroad a hundred years earlier. But many of them had returned to the old country due to the prejudice in the U.S.

Jackie walked us to the gate and I was afraid Jerry might chicken out at the last minute. I had to admit I was a little scared about my first few days alone with my son.

Instead, it was Jerry who comforted his mother. "It will be okay, Mom," he said to his crying mother.

"You'll be careful with him, right? Make sure you watch over him," Jackie said to me.

"Of course, I won't even let him fart in public."

Jerry immediately proved me wrong and my eyes began to water. I gave Jackie a hug as did Jerry and we were on our way.

***

We took off and Jerry was acting like he was on a ride with eyes closed until we got to 31,000 feet. I was glad I'd given him the window seat which I usually take.

"Your son's first flight? I remember my son's first time," the flight attendant said.

"Yeah, he's really enjoying himself and it's our first big trip together," I said, after hesitating to bask in the glory of her calling him my son.

Jerry told her about the World Series; making sure to bring up his favorite player.

"Yeah, I liked watching him play for the Dukes. I'm a big fan of Candy, too." She handed him some M & M's. Watching me for a sign of approval.

"It's okay. I'll probably steal them from him anyway," I said.

I got my first dirty look from Jerry but that changed quickly when I pointed out the Grand Canyon, quite a sight from the plane. As he was looking, I grabbed a few M & M's; my son didn't notice until I shoved them into my mouth.

I had to give him a quarter.

***

Jackie and Josie were busy cleaning Jerry's room while he was gone. "I sure miss him and it's only been a few hours," Josie said. "Do you think he'll be okay?"

"Those two are like two peas in a pod. I really miss Jerry, too, but I miss Jim as well. He's a little like a kid but I think he would give his life for Jerry," Jackie said.

245

"I didn't think it would happen but I'm actually a little jealous of Larry spending all this time with Jian. And I'm the one who set it up!"

"We'll see what happens when they come back but they have to make things look good."

But Josie had her doubts. "I dunno about her back story; She says she just came here to work but I've heard there's been a big influx of Chinese after the Tiananmen Square Massacre in June. A lot of them were revolutionaries."

"Even if she was, it would have been part of an Anti-Communist revolution and that would make us welcome her with open arms."

"Well, I'll welcome Larry back with open arms, but I sure hope his heart is still open to me."

"I know Jim's heart is still open and I think I'm going to ask him to move in when he comes back. I'm sure the blood test will show a match."

"And you think he'll say yes?"

Jackie explained to her sister how our conversations had gone and that even though we hadn't slept together recently, all was well.

***

Jerry went to the bathroom just after we landed in Vegas; half of the reason was probably his excitement over the view of the Strip as we were descending. We didn't have to change planes but decided to get out for the forty-five minutes or so that we'd be on the ground.

My first instinct was to head for the poker machines but then I remembered the little guy holding my arm. Jerry was having a positive effect on me already; I thought as I watched my brother and Jian put a twenty-dollar bill in a quarter slot machine.

And hit a four-hundred-dollar jackpot.

"Ready for another ride, Jerry? It's time to get back on the plane," I said.

"Yeah, you want some gum?" The novelty was already wearing off, or so I thought until Jerry asked when we could go back up again after landing in The City by the Bay.

Chapter 69

The Call of the Wild:

Jerry Chang's limo picked us up at the airport and took us on a roundabout route to his original restaurant in Chinatown. My son's eyes lit up as we went past the trolleys then up and down the hilly Lombard Street. We eventually flattened out to the Embarcadero close enough to get a whiff of Fisherman's Wharf.

Jerry was taking in the sights and smells all the way, including the smell of the chopped liver our driver was eating with crackers. All the way to the restaurant.

"So I hear your name is Jerry just like mine," the restaurateur said to my son after giving his niece a hug. "You must be very hungry after your trip, Jerry."

"I can use chopsticks," Jerry Chavez said. "And I am ready now."

We all got a good laugh. "He really has been practicing," I said. "Thank you so much for giving us this opportunity."

"Oh, think nothing of it. It is very nice to meet Jian's new family," Mr. Chang said. "Come here into our private room where my chefs will prepare a traditional Chinese dinner for you."

The restaurant had beautiful murals on the wall and other art on bamboo as well as some pieces which appeared to be real jade. Larry touched a frog and, by the look on his face, I could tell that it was certainly not plastic.

"Go ahead, everybody should touch the frog for good luck," Jian said.

"You have a beautiful place here, Mr. Chang," Larry said as we sat down to the ornately wood carved table and chairs with 1930's chandelier hanging above. It was set with pure crystal glasses and porcelain dishes along with ivory chopsticks.

"Thank you…but you can call me Uncle Jerry," our host said.

Little Jerry was looking at the chopsticks and trying to hold onto them. "These are slippery, not like the wood ones."

"We can get you a fork and spoon but no knives are allowed on a Chinese table," Chang said. "Or you can try to dip it in water to make it hold better."

My son looked up at me, obviously puzzled because water always made things more slippery. "Just try it," I told him.

We ate our dinner of Xiao Long Bao, Mapo Tofu, Jellyfish and 1,000-year-old eggs along with several other dishes and lots of rice washed down with a white liquor, Moutai baijiu. We were all feeling good, and sated besides, with only enough energy to figure out how to get to the redwood forest and Jack London Square in Oakland.

It was a lifelong dream of mine to see the redwoods of California and I had read both White Fang and The Call of the Wild as a kid. I had enjoyed them almost as much as The Jungle Books but there was no Rudyard Kipling Park in Oakland. We would start the day off at its All Good Bakery, famous due to its Black Panther roots but also known for excellent sweets.

**

Jerry was up early the next morning and I turned on the TV in the bedroom of Jerry Chang's home so the little guy could watch some cartoons. I called Don up in the meantime since I knew everyone else would be sleeping in due to the liquor.

"So, how's Frisco so far?"

"Pretty good, we just got a quick drive around and a great traditional Chinese meal last night. But Jerry's having a great time; especially on the plane. How's the new place shaping up?"

"Coming along and I love my job." My brother was executive chef of a little B & B called The Vermont Marble Inn with rooms themed on different British authors.

"Hey, have you seen anything of our illustrious fairy godfather?"

"No, why are you worried about that jerk?"

"He's kind of an ass but he did help me to find Larry. I'm not really worried…he can take care of himself. Matter of fact that's what he's usually doing."

"So what's the plan today before the game?"

I ran down our plan for the day and Don warned me to get back across to Frisco and Candlestick Park early. "There's a lot of traffic. I know you tend to get carried away when you're sightseeing but have fun at the game."

"It's gonna be great; Jerry's so easy to take care of. We had our blood tests yesterday and hope to have some results soon but I know already. Take care."

I heard the phone ring and somebody called upstairs to say that it was for me. It was Jackie asking how I was feeling this morning; apparently I'd called her when I was drunk last night.

She wanted to talk to her son and I got Jerry away from the TV long enough to say hello to his mother. He handed the phone back to me.

"Jerry seems to be doing well; he said he slept well and ate enough that he's not even hungry yet today." You could hear a little something in her voice. I knew she was disappointed that he didn't miss her more.

"Yeah, we ate…and drank well last night. I mean, er, everybody but Jerry drank well. He's a pretty low-maintenance kid."

"Well, Josie and I tried hard…I'm glad you guys are getting along. Say, how would you feel about moving in once you get your stuff back to Albuquerque? Josie's moving out."

"That would be great but I've hardly lived in an apartment. I love you and could live in an oversized refrigerator box with you and be happy."

"Hey, I have a call from Lobo Labs coming in and I love you, too."

"The lab…already. Wow!"

249

It turned out the lab was calling for my number since they had to talk to me. After being told that I needed a secretary, I found out they had expedited the blood test since it looked like there was a chance of a mix-up the first time.

"Mr. Goodman, you are a paternal match to Jerry Chavez," the nurse said.

"Oh…thank you, thank you, thank you. I knew it all along." But I didn't dare try to explain it to Jerry without his mother there. I did, however, call Jackie right back to give her the confirmation. Everybody else was waking up so it was time to go and I bade Jackie farewell until tomorrow night.

I was excited to see one of my favorite authors in a little while.

Chapter 70

A Day to Remember, A Day to Forget:

We tried to leave after everyone had a quick shower but Jerry's staff had prepared some Chinese pastries for our breakfast. Red bean paste, pineapple and cherry-filled baozi plus some lotus seed mooncakes, which we ate in the same private room. Then there was the ever-present chopped liver which Jimmy seemed to be the only one to partake of.

Jerry Chang warned us not to eat too quickly since it was bad for the digestion but the combination of good food and the great adventure awaiting us kept us only talking between bites. We ate what we could, took a few pastries with us since we wouldn't have time for lunch (it was already 10 AM) and told our host we would meet him at Candlestick Park.

We took the limo again. Jimmy, who had brought us from the airport the day before, was our driver. Not very far from Chinatown, I-80 crossed the bay to Oakland and both locations I wanted to check out were right off another artery. Redwoods Regional Park was a little farther so we would start there and come to Jack London Square on the way back.

"Wow, look at all this water," Jerry said. He had never been over a bridge like that before.

Jimmy knew a lot about the bridge and its history as well as the surrounding area. Jerry listened intently while most of what he was

251

saying went in one of my ears and out the other since I could only think of seeing the world's tallest trees. I had dreamed of seeing them since I was little but only recently learned that sequoias and redwoods were actually different trees.

The sequoias, which I probably wouldn't see on this trip, were older plus a little shorter and a lot wider than the coastal redwoods. The trees were kind of like humans in the respect that they lost height and gained weight as they aged.

As my brother Don had predicted, we kind of lost track of time while walking through the redwoods taking pictures and hiding behind trees. By the time we left, around 2 PM, we would barely have time to pose with the Jack London statue and get to the sold-out baseball game by 4 PM, an hour before the first pitch.

Jimmy warned us about how the traffic might start up around 3 PM, so he advised going straight back to the stadium. But I was bound and determined to see the statue of one of my favorite writers who also wrote some more adult books like *John Barleycorn*. The Traffic version of the English folk song that London's book was named after was playing in my head while Jimmy talked and drove, turning on the radio to the same version.

"Well, I guess Traffic started earlier today," I joked, not thinking our driver would get it.

Apparently, the local classic rock station had a pre-rush hour segment of Traffic every Tuesday. Jimmy and I sang in stereo, "John Barleycorn must die."

"It's 2:30 already; maybe we should go straight back to Frisco," I said to Jimmy but loud enough for everyone else to hear. "Besides, you must be running low on chopped liver and Ritz crackers by now. Where'd you ever get hooked on that?"

Jimmy replied that a Jewish family who often came to the Chinese restaurant started bringing him *noshes* every time they got Peking duck. "It was either chopped liver or pickled herring," He could tell that Larry and I could relate to that dilemma — the lesser of two evils.

252

The vote was close but it was three to two that we go to Jack London Square. I should have remembered that Larry liked the author as well.

Luckily, Jimmy knew right where the statue was and pulled up as close to it as he could with the car. We ran over to it and took some pictures of each other, then were back on our way inside of five minutes.

But it was already too late; it was as if someone were giving away box seats for the Series starting at 3:01 PM. We got on I-880 and it looked nothing like the fast-moving five-lane highway that we'd come in on.

All we could do is pray that things would open up but Jimmy wasn't confident. He called his boss on the phone to tell him of the delay and Jerry was obviously yelling at him for the problem. He did also own a forty-foot boat but Jimmy usually drove that so Jerry wasn't sure that he'd be able to get it going and bring everyone back in time for the game.

We talked about baseball and debated whether the Giants or Athletics would win; luckily, we still had the pastries and Jimmy had baijiu to wash it down. Little Jerry laid down after eating a little too much and we all were still drinking when we passed by the clock at 4:35 PM.

We were getting closer to the bridge but still wouldn't be able to make it in time for the first pitch. Right now, with the liquor flowing, that didn't seem to matter that much. Until I looked at my son, that is.

He was fast asleep but I was sure he was dreaming about the baseball game and seeing Candy Maldonado belt a home run to give the home team a lead in the bottom of the ninth.

It was 5:00 PM and Jimmy turned the game on the TV in the back of the limo. But with opening ceremonies, the first pitch had yet to be thrown by 5:04.

But something else was happening as the TV cameras began shaking and the road beneath us began to rumble. Within a few seconds, the limo was hanging by a bent bumper and we were watching

253

people in crushed cars below and others hanging above I-880 like something out of a horror movie. People in blue-collar uniforms were coming to help but it looked like the odds were overwhelmingly against them getting to us in time.

We tried to shield Jerry's eyes from seeing the carnage around us. It appeared as if Jimmy had been crushed by the steering wheel and his blood was now running from the front seat to the back seat. While it was obvious that our driver was gone, Larry asked if everyone else was alright and a couple of them had shut down from shock already.

"Now, Jerry, I want you to be a brave little guy. If you do that, I think we can get you out of here," Larry told his nephew, who was crying. Understandably, for the first time on the trip, he was calling for his mother and looking for her help from 1,000 miles away.

They could just imagine what Jackie would be going through if she knew what was happening. That was why Larry would try to get his nephew out through the broken windshield to where Jerry could climb over the hood using seatbelts strung together.

The new groom was thinking to himself that he'd been destined to die ten years ago on that beach and now it was finally going to happen. But at least he could do something good before the car fell into the filled marshland far below and the intermittent, ominous creaking was a hint that such a moment was not far away.

He got the Cub Scout knife, the only thing he still had from his childhood, out of his pocket and began cutting the seat belts from their holders. Jian tied them together until they were about ten feet long but then we realized that there was another problem.

"This thing is not going to attach itself to the front of the car," Larry said. The creaking became a little more consistent — a warning that time was even more of the essence.

Jian had been watching *MacGyver* over the last few years as part of an effort to learn English. But she put her acquired skills to good use by bending a coat hanger and putting it through the notch of the seatbelt. "That could hopefully catch the little piece of bridge sticking out right there," Jian said and as she pointed there was another loud creak.

"Let's go for it," Larry said. He was putting his shirt over Jerry's face so he couldn't look out. "Just keep holding onto this (the seatbelt) and climbing."

"Just like I climb a tree?"

"Yeah. You ready?" Larry gave him an initial push up to the front seat but the belt broke just as the car let loose.

The arm came reaching out and was only able to save three of them. Jerry first, then Jian and then Larry. Larry looked down and his brother's body had disappeared from the back seat.

But he was relieved when he saw Jim on top once he got there. "How…what the hell…wha…," Larry tried to get out a full sentence.

The smell of chopped liver not only drowned the stench of the carnage but also pointed to who our new guardian angel was. A lone crow feasted on the Ritz cracker crumbs along the crumbled roadway.

If you have a clue about Larry's whereabouts, please email findinglarry63@gmail.com to qualify for the reward. If your tip leads to finding out what happened to my brother, you will be given an award based on a percentage of the book's sales. Otherwise, a percentage will go to a missing persons charity.